Flash Flood

CHRIS RYAN

RED FOX

FLASH FLOOD
A RED FOX BOOK 978 0 099 48863 7 (from January 2007)
0 099 48863 9

First published in Great Britain by Red Fox,
an imprint of Random House Children's Books

This edition published 2006

1 3 5 7 9 10 8 6 4 2

Papers used by Random House Children's Books are natural,
recyclable products made from wood grown in sustainable forests.
The manufacturing processes conform to the environmental
regulations of the country of origin.

Set in Sabon

Red Fox Books are published by Random House Children's Books,
61-63 Uxbridge Road, London W5 5SA,
a division of The Random House Group Ltd,
in Australia by Random House Australia (Pty) Ltd,
20 Alfred Street, Milsons Point, Sydney, NSW 2061, Australia,
in New Zealand by Random House New Zealand Ltd,
18 Poland Road, Glenfield, Auckland 10, New Zealand,
and in South Africa by Random House (Pty) Ltd,
Isle of Houghton, Corner Boundary Road & Carse O'Gowrie,
Houghton 2198, South Africa

THE RANDOM HOUSE GROUP Limited Reg. No. 954009

www.kidsatrandomhouse.co.uk

A CIP catalogue record for this book is available from the British Library.

Printed and bound in Great Britain by
Cox & Wyman Ltd, Reading, Berkshire

A CODE RED ADVENTURE

Location: London

'I know you're probably sick of environmentalists like me banging on about global warming. The sea level rising and all that rubbish. But think of it this way. You know the Thames Barrier? You know that without it a lot of central London would be under water? Well, in twenty-five years' time, if you don't build a much bigger Thames Barrier, London will be under water anyway. That's what rising sea levels mean.

'Twenty-five years; it's not long, is it? Or, if you're really unlucky with the weather, it could be twenty-five minutes.'

Dr Bel Kelland, environmentalist,
News Focus, August 2006

Chapter One

'This is crap, this train,' said the youth with the pierced eyebrow, and kicked the door next to his seat. It was one of the old-type trains with doors that slam shut, and when he kicked it the window rattled.

A woman sitting on the end of the row with a leather holdall on her knee jumped at the sound and looked annoyed. The youth's two friends, both wearing hoodies and a variety of face piercings, saw her reaction and snorted with laughter. They were about sixteen, they were bored, and they were determined to make everyone else suffer too.

Like everyone else in the carriage, Ben and Rachel

tried to ignore them. The train journey was unpleasant enough as it was. Ever since they had got on at their home town of Macclesfield in Cheshire it had been stop-start all the way. Now it was stop. Heavy rain had caused flooding and signal failures. The carriage smelled of wet raincoats and damp seats; the floor was wet from dripping umbrellas. Some people were wearing wellington boots. You could hardly believe it was the first week of August.

Everyone was fed up, wondering when the train was going to move again. Ben Tracey – dark blond hair, thoughtful face, thirteen years old but looked older – was going to London to spend the day with his mother. His parents were separated and he didn't get to see his mother very often because she travelled a lot. Twenty-two-year-old Rachel, his next-door neighbour, was fully made up and dressed much more smartly than Ben. She was accompanying him as far as Milton Keynes, where she had a job interview. She'd already had to phone to tell them she'd be late. Everyone in the carriage was sitting and gritting their teeth, or looking out at the relentless rain, which lashed the windows like a storm at sea.

'I said this train's *crap*,' said Pierced Eyebrow, and kicked the door again. This time he kicked harder and the window slipped down in the frame. Water dribbled in through the gap and down the window, leaving streaks in the black grime and pooling on the dirty floor.

His two friends laughed. 'Hey, man, you've broken it.' One of them scratched his nose, making the piercing he'd got there jiggle up and down. He noticed the woman with the holdall looking at it distastefully. He stuck his finger into the nostril and waggled the stud from inside like someone making a teddy bear wave. 'Hey, Grandma, do you like my piercing?'

She looked pointedly the other way, out of the window.

Pierced Eyebrow fished in his pocket. He brought out a marker pen and wrote an unreadable signature in big letters on the glass, then sat back grinning.

Through the open window they could hear the sound of a train approaching. Pierced Nose got up, stuck his head out and yelled at the train.

'Any chance of a lift, mate?' His last word was swallowed up by the thunder of the train approaching. Pierced Eyebrow and his companion, who had a septic-looking piercing through his top lip, grabbed Nose's Abercrombie hoodie and yanked him back in.

The train bowled past close to the windows; the clearance couldn't have been more than half a metre.

The three youths looked shaken for a moment, then started to laugh. Pierced Nose shook the rain out of his hair. 'Hey, man, that was cool – you gotta try it.'

Septic Lip stood up and stuck his head out of the window. 'There's another one coming. Watch this.' He pushed the window all the way down and leaned his whole upper body out, waving with both arms while the train drummed closer. 'Woo-hoo!' he called.

Now everyone in the carriage was staring at them. This train was going a lot faster; it was an inter-city. They could feel it shaking the floor of the carriage. Its horn blared.

'Woo-hoo!' called Septic Lip, his arms waving wildly out of the window. Nose and Eyebrow grabbed the back of his jeans and pulled him in. The train passed in a blur of blue and white. The shock wave shook the stationary carriage from side to side.

The youths were laughing. Septic clutched at Eyebrow's sweatshirt and pushed him towards the window. 'Come on, man: your turn.'

Eyebrow wasn't going to stick his head out without the audience's attention. He looked around at the rest of the passengers to see how well the show was going down. Ben thought he looked as if he expected some kind of praise for being so brave.

Pierced Nose noticed Ben's expression. 'What are you looking at?'

Rachel had been looking too. She looked away immediately the youth started talking to them. But Ben held his gaze. 'Be careful,' he said.

Now the other people in the carriage were looking at Ben.

'Go back to reading *Harry Potter*,' said Eyebrow. He turned away and looked out of the window, planning when he'd stick his head through. When he glanced back, Ben was still looking at him.

'What?' he said.

'Well, it's just that I had this friend . . .' Ben said. 'But go ahead, it's your life.' He turned back to the novel he'd been reading.

Pierced Eyebrow couldn't stand losing his audience's attention. That wasn't meant to happen. Especially as that audience was now paying more attention to Ben than to him. He walked over to Ben. 'Yeah? And what are you saying?'

Ben put his bookmark carefully back in his book before looking up at Pierced Eyebrow. 'He was a good friend too. I'd known him for years.'

'That's lovely,' said Eyebrow. 'Very touching.'

Ben nodded, as though considering the matter, but said nothing. He opened his book again to resume reading.

Eyebrow looked irritated. 'And . . . ? Your point is . . . ?'

Ben gave a sigh and carefully replaced his bookmark. He definitely had Eyebrow's attention now: he could take all the time he wanted.

'It was very sad. He got on a train – one of the old ones with windows like this. He'd had a burger at a stall in the station – you know how they can be a bit dodgy. Well, he started feeling sick, which serves him right really for eating such rubbish.' Ben paused again.

'Come on, I haven't got all day,' said Eyebrow, but Ben wasn't to be hurried.

'There was a woman sitting next to him,' said Ben, 'and my friend thought, I'm going to be sick, what shall I do? I can't be sick on her. But he couldn't stop it, so he put his head out of the window.'

Septic and Nose looked at Ben as if they suspected the story was about to turn into a joke and make them look foolish. But they couldn't help but listen.

'And then what?' said Eyebrow testily.

'A train came the other way and took the top of his head off. Like an egg.' Ben mimed it, one hand slicing over the top of the other.

For a split second the look on the youths' faces was shocked. Then they covered it up with bluster.

'Yeah, right,' sneered Nose. Eyebrow glanced towards the window as though he was still going to take his turn playing chicken with the next express, but Ben noticed he didn't put his head out again.

Ben opened his book and scanned the pages, as if taking time to look for the bit he'd been reading. 'But you go ahead. Carry on doing what you're doing.'

Rachel got a magazine out of her bag and held it up in front of her face to stop herself laughing. She could see the dilemma clearly. The youths were shaken, but they didn't want to show it or they would look stupid. But they certainly no longer felt like sticking their heads out of the window. Eyebrow and Nose fidgeted, and Septic had put up his sopping wet hood and was trying to use it to dry off his short spiky hair. With just a well-chosen story, thirteen-year-old Ben had completely disarmed them.

She couldn't help but admire him. If she'd been there on her own she'd have sat there quietly and hoped the lads would disappear; she'd never have had the guts to say anything. But then, Ben's mother was the environmental campaigner Dr Bel Kelland, and often appeared live on television and had arguments with world leaders and the chairmen of big corporations. Maybe that's where he got his confidence. He certainly didn't get it from his father, Russell Tracey, who was a brilliant scientist but rather shy.

'Man, it's boring in here,' said Pierced Eyebrow. 'Let's go and find somewhere more interesting.' He swaggered up to the doors leading to the next carriage and pushed through. The others followed him.

Rachel put down her magazine. 'That was an interesting story. Who was the friend?'

'My cousin Jack,' said Ben. 'And he wasn't that polite. He threw up over the woman.'

Rachel laughed. 'Is that how your mother deals with troublesome people?' She was rather in awe of Ben's mother, and fascinated. Bel travelled the world, making her mark. When the tsunami struck South East Asia in 2004 she was filmed in the devastated villages, warning politicians and the public alike that this was the kind of thing that happened when you didn't look after your planet. With her slight figure, straight red hair and trademark crumpled safari shirt, she was instantly recognizable. No wonder she had outgrown an insignificant town in the north-west like Macclesfield.

'No,' said Ben. 'My mother would have waded in and had a fight. It would be very embarrassing.'

'Your dad's not like that at all.'

'Yeah. If Dad had been here too he'd have sat in the corner and fumed in silence.'

'How did they ever get together?'

'Beats me.'

The train began to move again, slowly, painfully. The guard spoke over the tannoy. '*Ladies and gentlemen, we are now on the move again. We're running forty-five minutes late. But just to cheer you up, the weather in London isn't any better than the weather here.*'

Around the carriage, people sighed, looked at their watches and flipped open their phones. They were thoroughly fed up with all this rain.

Chapter Two

The groundsman at Lord's Cricket Ground in north-west London looked miserably into the grey sky. The rain pounded on his umbrella as if it was a drum; the water ran off the edges like a cascade. Most of the summer had been like this. The Wimbledon tennis championships had dragged out to four weeks instead of two, in order to get enough dry days to play all the matches. If the weather didn't improve, it looked as though the summer's cricket might never start at all.

He put the collar of his Barbour up and stepped onto the pitch. The grass was so soggy, his feet sank in; it was like standing on a wet sponge. Even if the rain stopped, it would be a good few days before play was possible. But there was no let-up forecast.

The drumming on the top of his umbrella became louder, as though the clouds had detected his thoughts and were offended by them. Thunder rumbled out of the glowering sky. Now a storm was coming too.

He decided there was no point in staying. There wasn't any work he could do today. He squelched off the grass, grateful when his feet met the solid tarmac of the car park. The rain was so hard it was hopping off the asphalt like jumping beans.

The groundsman opened the door of his car, pulled his Barbour off and bundled it, dripping, into the passenger seat, then scrambled in.

He couldn't see through the windscreen. The rain was so hard it blurred it as though the glass was melting. He started the engine and put the wipers on. Even on extra fast they struggled to create a clear space he could see through. He edged along the drive and pulled out into St John's Wood Road.

The engine stalled, which it often did. His car didn't like wet weather. As he pulled the handbrake on and turned the ignition key again, he caught a glimpse of looming headlights behind. There was a wail of a horn and a screech of tyres. A big silver saloon, travelling too fast, aquaplaned on the road and hit his rear bumper with a dull crunch.

For a few nanoseconds he got a clear view through the rear window of the driver of the car getting wearily out, then the rain blurred the glass again.

Great. Just what he needed.

Ensign Henrik peered through the windscreen on the bridge of the ship. The wipers could barely keep up with the volume of water streaming down the glass.

Outside was the grey choppy surface of the river Thames. It blended into the brooding grey of the sky. From time to time he could see the lights of boats in the distance, pinpricks of red bobbing up and down on the choppy waters.

'You're doing fine,' said a voice behind him. The captain leaned back in his chair and took a drag on his cigarette. 'Just keep her steady. Remember you've got a full load.'

The *Agnetha* was a big ship, about the length of a football pitch from bow to stern. She was also old and took some careful handling. Particularly with several hundred tonnes of aggregates in the hold, which slowed down the responsiveness of the controls so much it was as if the ship had gone to sleep. Henrik had piloted her before, but that was only on the return journey, when she was empty. Today he was taking her all the way from the port of Hango, on the southernmost tip of Finland, to the deep-water terminals at Greenwich docks.

What a day he'd picked. This weather was terrible; he could hardly see a thing. At least it wasn't far now to their destination.

He looked to the shores of the Thames on either side of him. They were virtually invisible. There were lights on the banks but they were blurred, as though the windows had been smeared with Vaseline. His own masthead light, the length of a football pitch away at the front of the boat, had disappeared into the murk. Even the sound of the engines, usually a low throbbing hum, was drowned out by the relentless quantities of rain drumming on the metal roof of the bridge.

'Watch out! Hard right!' Henrik saw a pinprick of

light right at the very corner on the radar display. Instantly the captain was standing over him, pulling the steering column hard to the right. The boat outside looked as if it was still some distance away. On the radar, it blipped slowly to the edge of the display and disappeared as the *Agnetha* turned. The captain stepped back again but he watched the radar closely for a few more anxious moments. Then he sank back into his chair.

'You need to give her far more time to turn when she's loaded like this,' he said.

Henrik nodded, chastened. 'But we didn't hear the collision alarm.'

'If we hear the alarm when we're fully laden it's too late,' was the acerbic reply.

The captain was looking tired, his elbow resting on the arm of his chair, his forehead resting on his hand. The cigarette lay forgotten, its smoke curling into a grey column in the air while the captain recovered from the shock. Henrik felt ashamed. They must have had a close call.

Henrik turned back, checked the instruments, looked at the radar very closely. He wouldn't make that mistake again. The river was still wide at this point, almost like a big lake. But the closer they got to Greenwich, the more it narrowed and the more hazards there were to navigate. This journey would only get more tricky.

When he next looked round at the captain, he got a shock. The captain was slumped in the chair, his right arm dangling on the ground like an ape's. He was twitching as though he was trying to get up but had no control over his body.

The cigarette fell from the fingers of his left hand. He didn't move to pick it up.

Henrik moved quickly over to him. 'Sir? Sir, are you all right?'

The captain tried to move. Again he only managed a fitful jerk, as if the swinging arm was a lead weight keeping him down.

'Sir, what's the matter?'

'I can't move. I can't see. Help me.'

Henrik wasn't sure if he'd heard him right. The captain's voice was slurred, as if he'd just been to the dentist. 'You can't see?'

The captain was staring ahead. He blinked as if he

was trying to clear his vision. 'I can't see.' He tried to shake his head but he only managed another twitch. One side of his mouth didn't seem to be working.

Henrik suddenly realized that the captain's strange behaviour reminded him of his grandmother after she had had a stroke.

He reached towards a big button on the console. 'Emergency, emergency, first aider needed on the bridge! Hello?'

And then he heard a sound he didn't want to hear. A wail like a siren.

The collision alarm.

Henrik looked at the radar. A big glowing blob showed at the top of the screen.

A voice answered him. 'Henrik? What's the matter?'

'Captain needs help. I think he's having a stroke.' Henrik steered hard right. It didn't stop the collision alarm. Maybe it would stop in a moment. He peered out of the window but could see nothing – just the grey rain and the far-off twinkle of lights through Vaseline.

'Keep his airway open,' said the medical officer. 'I'm on my way up.'

Henrik dropped down on one knee beside the captain. The captain stared at him, his watery blue eyes big and scared. He was breathing fast, like he'd run a race. But he was still breathing.

Henrik patted him gently on the shoulder. 'They're on their way, sir.' He went back to the radar again. The big glowing blob looked closer.

Another voice came out of the console. 'Henrik? What's going on up there? The collision alarm's going off. That's the Thames Barrier out there.' It was the guys in the radio room.

'Can you get me a helmsman?' said Henrik. 'We're in trouble up here.'

The hatch from the stairwell opened. 'Where is he?' It was the medical officer.

Just as he was starting to examine the captain, they heard a great grinding crash. Henrik was thrown to the floor and rolled into a corner. He stopped when he hit the wall and looked up groggily. The floor was at a crazy angle and the control panel was alive with red lights like a Christmas tree. The captain had tumbled out of the chair and was lying on the floor, mumbling. The medical officer had been thrown into the wall.

His head was gushing blood. Alarms and sirens wailed around him like wounded animals.

In the Thames Barrier control centre on the south bank of the Thames, the air was also wailing with alarms. Looking through the window, the engineer could scarcely believe what he had seen. Everything had been normal, the row of silver metal shells containing the machinery that raised the flood gates stretching across the river like a chain of silver hoods. A large container ship had been coming towards them, but these vessels usually judged the width of the navigation channels just right.

However, this one had rammed into the concrete plinth at the waterline, ridden up it like a car mounting a pavement, and penetrated the barrier like a spear.

The engineer was so stunned that for a few moments he stood looking at it, at the metallic hood buckled like tinfoil, the sparks spewing like fireworks into the rain and the hulk of the ship still shuddering from the impact.

Then he snatched up the telephone. 'Code Red! Code Red! The Barrier is out of action!'

Chapter Three

The rain was still coming down hard, making the roofs look glossy and grim. The guard's voice came over the tannoy. '*Ladies and gentlemen, we are arriving at Milton Keynes. Thank you for travelling with us today. Please be careful on the wet platforms.*'

The train stopped. Rachel got to her feet and went to the door. The window had never properly closed again after the youths had kicked it. Rain was trickling down the inside, making a puddle on the floor and streaking paths through the graffiti they had left.

Rachel gave Ben a hug. 'Try to stay out of trouble.'

She put up her hood and stepped down. The platform was swimming with water.

Ben handed her her bag. 'Good luck with the interview.'

'Have a lovely day with your mum.' Rachel slammed the door and splashed away on tiptoe.

As the train pulled away, Ben looked at his watch. Another three-quarters of an hour and he should be in Euston, then he would get a Tube to meet Bel. He got out his phone. He'd better let his mum know how long he would be.

He got her message service: *'Life's too short for regrets. This is Bel. Say what you need to say.'*

Typical Bel: a bit abrasive, a bit embarrassing. He wished she'd change that message.

'I can see your eyes are starting to glaze over. Yeah, you know all about global warming. People have been talking about it for years. Everyone in this room knows all that stuff. We've burned too much fossil fuel over the years so now we're getting floods, severe storms and all that. Silly us . . . blah blah blah . . . global warming, the same old record. When I was at school in the seventies people were talking about it. And still it seems nothing has changed.'

In the conference centre in Whitehall, Bel stood at the lectern. Her speech was on notes in front of her, but she didn't refer to them. Auburn hair fell in a neat straight curtain to her shoulders; her clear blue eyes searched the faces in front of her. She was wearing a dark purple suit that was slightly crumpled, as if looking smart didn't come easily to her. Her audience was made up of industry leaders, government representatives and journalists. Some of them were taking notes, others were looking at her patiently. A good half of them had detached expressions – they looked as if they were thinking about something else: possibly the buffet lunch that waited under clingfilm on the platters at the back of the room.

Rain splashed against the big windows of the conference centre, forming a constant hiss behind Bel's voice, like interference on a radio. Outside, the traffic rumbled to and from Trafalgar Square, a blur of red brake lights and white headlights.

It was lunch time but it was dark enough to be dusk.

Bel continued. 'We talk about terrorism being the biggest threat facing us today. We put millions of pounds into making our airport security safer, putting more police on the streets, upgrading surveillance in our cities. About three thousand people died in the Twin Towers, less than a hundred died in the bombing attempts on London. But thirty thousand people died in the earthquake in Iran and two hundred and eighty-three thousand died in the tsunami in South East Asia.' She paused and searched the faces of the people in the front row. 'These are the casualties nature can inflict in a war. And it *is* a war.'

The journalists had woken up and were scribbling again. *Nature at war*: that was a good quote. That would go in the headlines this evening.

One of the journalists put his hand up. 'Should the government have more green policies?'

Bel looked at him incredulously. 'That has to be the dumbest question of the day. What do you think?' She waved her hand at the rainy street outside. 'Look at it out there. It's more like the tropics than London. Of course they should have more green policies. They should have had them twenty years ago. Look, we shouldn't have called it global warming – it sounds too nice. Warm is comfortable, warm is cuddly. Well, global warming isn't comfortable or cuddly; it isn't even warm. The polar ice caps start melting. Then the Gulf Stream no longer protects us. You know what it's like in New York in winter? Freezing. Miserable. You know what it's like in Siberia in winter? Don't even go there. That's what this country will be like if the Gulf Stream stops coming our way. The last thing it will be is warm.'

An official wearing a conference organizer's badge stepped forward from the wings. 'Ladies and gentlemen, that was Dr Bel Kelland from the environmental organization Fragile Planet. Now we'll break for lunch.'

Bel picked up her papers and moved away from the lectern. The audience were already on their feet, heading resolutely for lunch. Bel could feel their relief as they were finally released, like school children waiting for the lesson to end. She felt irritated with them, but didn't have time to indulge it. She had to be somewhere else. Ben would be arriving soon.

She hurried off the stage and started to make her way towards the doors at the back of the room. She zipped along a row of seats, trying to get ahead of the lunch crowd, and ran into a journalist with a scraped-back ponytail who was holding out a Dictaphone.

'Dr Kelland, would now be a good time for our interview?' Her manicured finger was hovering over the record button.

Bel looked at her watch. 'Not really. I'm rushing to meet my son. Send me an e-mail at the office.' She pressed a business card into the journalist's hand, pushed aside some chairs and nipped through to another row.

She was nearly at the door when a man in a baggy dark suit intercepted her. His greying hair stuck up like a backcombed badger.

'Hi, Clive,' she said. Clive Brooks worked in the Department of the Environment.

'Bel. Terrific speech.' He folded his arms across his chest and stroked his chin, as if he had all the time in the world.

Bel looked at her watch irritably. She knew he wouldn't have liked her speech at all. 'Sorry, Clive, I've got to rush.'

'We're just on our way to a briefing with the Prime Minister of Canada. He's asked to meet you.'

Bel was genuinely surprised. 'I'd love to, Clive. Can you arrange it? Only I've got an appointment.'

'He's flying out tomorrow. It'll have to be now. A car's taking us to the Cabinet Office. You can hitch a ride with us if you want.'

That stopped Bel in her tracks. She didn't get offers like that very often. The decision was made in an instant. She got out her phone. 'Give me five minutes. I've just got to rearrange something.'

Bel walked out to the foyer, found a quiet corner and dialled. 'Cally? Can you do me a favour? Ben's coming down and I'm stuck in a meeting. Can you amuse him for a while?'

A few minutes later, she turned and made her way back towards Clive Brooks. As she did so, she noticed that the floor was becoming ever more wet and slippery. It was as if the rain was slowly coming in, on people's shoes, on their umbrellas, on their dripping coats. Like a tide slowly creeping into the building.

The Thames Barrier was a huge structure. The gap between each of the silver-coloured hoods was as wide as the central deck of Tower Bridge, to allow ships to pass through. The hoods themselves stood on solid concrete islands. Each was as tall as a five-storey building and was coated with steel. But the crashed container ship was also a giant. Its living quarters were even taller than the steel shells and its prow had crushed the metal like a car running over a drinks can.

Two rescue boats were making their way away from the crash site. They looked like tiny specks tossing about on the rough water.

Inside the control room, the engineers were trying to handle the emergency. Warning lights blinked on the operating console. On the wall was a Perspex diagram of the barrier; it was covered in lights and every one of them was winking red.

The duty controller was getting a radio update from the rescue boats outside. 'We've got the crew off and the captain's on his way to hospital but we can't move the ship. She was carrying a full load. It's going to take about ten tugs to pull her away. Over.'

'Well, get started,' replied the controller, exasperated. 'What are you waiting for? Over.'

'We've only got four tugs,' came the reply. 'We'll have to get in extra from Canvey Island. Over.'

'Get them as fast as you can. It's high tide in less than an hour. Over.'

An engineer in a yellow site hat and reflective safety vest was talking to the Meteorological Office on a mobile. With his other hand he was gesturing at the Thames Barrier controller.

The controller understood. He spoke to the team in the rescue boats. 'Mind out of the way, we're going to try raising the gates again.'

'Roger. Over and out.'

The controller nodded to the chief engineer at the control console, who hit the switch again. A great noise came from outside, like a giant machine starting. Outside on the river, in three of the four navigation channels, the giant steel gates began to rise out of the water. One by one they locked into position, in a carefully planned order so that they wouldn't disrupt the fast-flowing current and cause problems for shipping further up the river.

In the fourth navigation channel, next to the wreckage, there was a harsh grinding sound, like metal tearing.

The chief engineer shook his head and pressed another switch. The gates began to lower again. He turned to the controller. 'It's no use. Gate One doesn't move.'

'Can't we raise it manually?'

'No. The whole mechanism is smashed. It's just not responding.'

The engineer in the yellow reflective vest told the liaison officer at the Met. Office what had happened. 'The mechanism is completely crushed . . . No, not all the gates, just one of them.' A little pause, then he put his hand over the mouthpiece again and spoke to the room. 'They say, can't we just raise the other gates?'

The controller's response was instant. 'No. Give me the phone . . . Hi . . . Yes, this is the controller. We can't raise the gates if one of them doesn't work.'

The man at the Met. Office sounded frustrated and worried. 'We've had eight inches of rainfall in the past twenty-four hours. The same amount as fell in Boscastle before the floods there. We need the barrier. You'd better raise as much of it as you can.'

'Listen, I'm an engineer and I'm telling you it won't help – it will make it worse. It will force the water through the smaller opening, making it run faster – like putting it through a funnel. It also means that if we did – heaven forbid – get a flood, it would be even more destructive. We're better keeping the whole thing open and trying to get the repairs done as soon as possible.'

The Met. Office man made an exasperated noise. 'Can't we get a crane to raise the barrier? It's high tide in less than an hour.'

'There isn't a crane that can lift it.'

'There must be. There are marinas up the Thames with boat yards. They have cranes for lifting boats into dry docks.'

'A normal pleasure boat weighs a couple of tonnes. The Thames Barrier gates weigh three thousand seven hundred tonnes each. That's the weight of more than twenty double-decker buses. They're so heavy they had to be built in situ.'

The liaison officer tutted again. 'In that case, I'm calling the Department of the Environment to tell them we've got an emergency – a Code Red situation.' He rang off.

'That's what we told you fifteen minutes ago,' said the controller as he put down the phone.

Chapter Four

Ben got off the Tube train at Waterloo. Behind him a plump girl in trainers and short, spiky dark hair was struggling to get her case off. It didn't look heavy but one of its wheels had got stuck in the grooves of the carriage floor, and she was trying to balance a large shoulder bag on the other arm, which slipped every time she tried to move the case. People were pushing past her and glaring at her, as if she was obstructing them on purpose.

'Mind the doors,' called the tannoy. 'This train is ready to depart.'

The girl gave her case a harder yank, and staggered

as the weight of her other bag nearly overbalanced her. The doors started to close, then encountered the obstacle and rolled back open again.

The tannoy came back to life again. '*Would you please remove any obstruction from the doors. This train is ready to leave.*'

Ben went back, took hold of the handle of the big case and gave it a hefty tug. It came free and the train doors slid shut.

'Thanks,' said the girl.

'Pleasure,' said Ben. 'Do you need a hand up the stairs with it?'

The girl looked grateful. 'Oh, would you? That's very kind. I've had the journey from hell this morning.' Her Welsh accent was strong.

'So have I.' Ben grinned. As he carried the case up the stairs, he noticed the label attached to the handle: VICKY JAMES, 14 WEST STREET, LLANDUDNO. Another newcomer to the city.

They emerged in a big concourse. Corridors led off to other platforms, and at the far end were two long flights of escalators.

'Thanks, I can take it now,' said Vicky James. She

stopped, got a piece of paper out of her pocket and looked up at the exit signs, puzzled. 'I don't suppose you know which exit I take for St Thomas's Hospital?'

Ben shook his head. 'Afraid not. I'm new here too.'

Vicky took the handle of her suitcase. 'Not to worry – I'll find a policeman or something. Thanks again for your help.' She strode off purposefully, her case leaving dirty tracks on the wet floor.

Ben went in a different direction. As he came up the escalator, the station seemed to get wetter and wetter. People coming down were pushing hoods off their heads, shaking out umbrellas, shrugging their shoulders to get the sticky wet clothes off their skin, grateful for the warmth of the Tube station. There was a strong smell of wet coats.

Bel had phoned him just as he'd arrived at Euston. Now, instead of meeting her in Leicester Square, he was to go to the South Bank to meet her friend Cally, who worked for the oil company ArBonCo research-ing clean fuels. Then, at half past three, he was to make his way to meet Bel at a place they'd met at before – the Costa Coffee in Charing Cross Station. That didn't leave much time with her. He was booked on the 19.40 train back from Euston.

He was annoyed. He'd come all this way and now he had to make small talk with Cally for an hour and a half in the offices of a multinational oil company. That was typical of Bel – Ben could hear his father saying it now; all she ever thought about was her career. According to his dad, she cared more about endangered ecosystems than about her own flesh and blood. Right now, Ben was thinking that he might as well have stayed at home.

At the top of the escalator, the floor was swimming in dirty water. Ben skim-read the signs and saw that ArBonCo had its own exit. Outside, the rain was coming down like a curtain of water, hissing as it hit the road and the pavement. A woman hurried past him into the station, shoulders hunched with misery, her eyes panda-like with running mascara. Ben put his collar up, hoped the ArBonCo entrance wasn't far and ran outside. He spotted the glass revolving doors immediately and sprinted for them.

Inside, the doors sealed out the road noise like an airlock. A set of pale leather sofas was arranged around a Perspex display case containing models of oil rigs and drilling platforms. The foyer was a haven of white marble but, in the wet, it was like an ice rink. A number of yellow signs were arranged around the foyer, warning that the floor was slippery. The rain was creeping in under the doors, and the muddy footprints from people's shoes spoiled the impression of tidy corporate grandeur.

A curly-haired woman was waiting for him. Cally. She got up and embraced him warmly. 'Ben, lovely to see you. You've grown.'

Ben winced whenever adults said that to him. 'Hi, Cally.'

'Here, get that wet coat off. I'll sign you in and let's get something from the canteen. Are you hungry?'

They bought sandwiches from the canteen in the basement and then took the lift up to the top floor. The doors opened onto an enormous room. Floor-to-ceiling windows looked out at the top of a big Ferris wheel, 135 metres high: the London Eye.

'This is the viewing gallery,' said Cally proudly. 'It used to be open to the public until it became a security risk. So it's quite a privilege to come up here now. Not many people get to see this.'

Ben could think of more interesting attractions to visit on a day out in London – the London Eye itself, for instance – but he was too polite to say so. And he'd been on the London Eye the last time he was in London with Bel, so he'd actually seen the view before. 'Very nice,' he said.

While they ate their sandwiches Cally asked him questions about how he was doing at school. He noticed she didn't ask about his father. That didn't surprise him. Bel's friends and his dad's friends were poles apart. After ten minutes Cally looked at her watch. 'I'm afraid I've got to go to a meeting. I'm really sorry – I told your mum I'd try to get out of it, but I really do have to be there. If you need me I'll be in the conference room. It's next to the canteen.'

'I'll be fine,' said Ben.

'OK. I'll come and collect you in an hour.' She called the lift, stepped in with a wave and was gone. Now Ben was on his own.

Ben put his headphones in and switched on his personal radio/MP3 player. Looking around as he listened to the Kaiser Chiefs, he spotted a bronze plaque on a stand next to the window. He wandered over to look at it. Engraved on the plaque was a drawing of the skyline, with a key explaining the names of the various buildings that lined the river downstream from the ArBonCo Centre. Ben could make out the dome of St Paul's, dwarfed by the lipstick-shaped tower of the Gherkin building. He walked along the gallery to the end of the room. Another bronze plaque showed the map of the view from there: the Post Office Tower up to the north; the river curving away, under Westminster Bridge and Lambeth Bridge; the Houses of Parliament – that was presumably where Bel was at the moment. Probably haranguing another politician about global warming.

The back of the building looked all the way across the roofs to Sydenham Hill and the Crystal Palace television transmitter, its red light just a faint smudge against the heavy grey sky.

Bel must be delighted about the weather today: it was a big I-told-you-so for the politicians who denied that the climate was changing. As he looked down at the riverbanks, he could see how high the Thames was – well over the normal high-tide mark, as far as he could see.

Ben had done a full circuit and was back at the London Eye. Had it moved? Yes: the people in the red cagoules were now at one o'clock instead of twelve. The wheel went slowly, like the hour hand on a clock. Ben had spent the whole day so far watching time drag by. First on a train going nowhere, now killing time at the top of this building.

The Kaiser Chiefs track finished. Ben leaned on the guard rail and decided to see what the London radio stations were like. Usually he listened to his native Key 103 Radio in Manchester, but down here he could try Capital FM. He skipped through the stations, looking for the frequency, and got a short blast of the news on Radio Four. The announcer's voice made him think of home. His dad usually had it on while he was tinkering in his workshop. He listened for a moment:

'*Motoring organizations have issued a weather warning to drivers, warning them not to set out unless their journey is absolutely necessary. Several towns in the South West, including Boscastle which was devastated by flooding a few years ago, are on flood alert.*'

Ben found Capital. He found a chirpy female

presenter, but the message was the same. '*Don't travel by car unless it's absolutely necessary. The M25 is gridlocked after flooding at Wisley. This is Meena Chohan in the Flying Eye, with all the latest traffic news as it happens.*'

He tuned through the stations until he found one playing an Usher track. He looked out of the window to see how many more millimetres the London Eye had moved.

Suddenly something caught his attention down below.

The river.

One moment it was lapping at the walls of the Embankment. The next, it was rising, as though the water was swelling, like a bath filling too fast.

And it didn't stop.

It swallowed the walls of the Embankment on the north side and spilled over the banks on the south . . .

Chapter Five

Down on the street below, the pavements, dark grey with rain, seemed to dissolve as the water surged over them.

People who were out walking, heads down under hats and umbrellas, looked at the water swirling at their feet and started to run. They ran up the steps of the London Aquarium.

The water followed them. It flowed over the half-wall by the National Theatre and swirled around the deserted café, clattering the chairs together. It lapped at the theatre entrance, then swirled down the passageways between the buildings and out over the roads.

In moments it had covered the square of green grass in front of the entrance to the ArBonCo Centre. It crept over the road, choking an excavator so that it stalled with its arm poised in the air like a yellow claw. It gushed down the steps of the ArBonCo Centre and filled the sunken stepped area in front of the glass doors like a swimming pool.

On Ben's headphones the music continued. The radio station seemed unaware of the catastrophe. He took the phones out of his ears.

The noise from outside was deafening. There was a loud roar like an earthquake as the water slammed into the sides of buildings. Very faintly Ben could hear other noises too; the faintest of sounds that he thought might be screams.

Looking across the river, he saw that, over on the north bank, the road was invisible. The river was twice as wide as it had been, bordered now by the rows of buildings opposite. And still the water continued to rise.

Ben saw a set of binoculars on a stand next to the window. He grabbed them and put them to his eyes.

What he saw made him go cold all over.

A tourist stall by the London Eye buckled as he watched, its canvas roof collapsing. Policemen's helmets, Union Jack bowler hats, brightly coloured T-shirts and a host of souvenirs spread out in the water and were swept upriver in the strong current. Burger wrappers and cardboard coffee cups were flushed out of bins and set off in clusters.

More, larger debris followed: the wooden chairs that had been standing outside the theatre; books and trestle tables from a stall under Waterloo Bridge; placards from the National Film Theatre shop and menu boards from the restaurants.

A distinctive shape skimmed through the water. Ben tried to focus the binoculars on it, unable to believe his eyes. A long pale grey outline; a triangular fin like a sail. He saw an eye. And then the words: SEE THE TIGER SHARK AT THE LONDON AQUARIUM. Yes, he was indeed looking at a shark, but it was a cardboard cut-out.

He focused on the far side of the river again. What had happened to the vehicles that had been travelling along the Embankment? It was lunch time, and quite a few people had been hurrying along the pavement under their inadequate umbrellas. A frisson of horror went up his spine. He realized he could no longer see the front doors of the buildings opposite. He couldn't see the cars and lorries because the water had completely engulfed them. That must mean the water was at least two metres deep on the Embankment. Probably three metres, because it was nearly up to the first-floor windows of the white building opposite.

Then Ben noticed the top of a double-decker bus sailing sideways past the white building. Only the red rectangle of its roof was visible; the rest was submerged.

Ben was amazed by the speed at which the flood waters had surged up. In only a matter of seconds, it seemed, they had risen up over the Embankment walls and totally covered the road above.

And then he began to see the people – helpless shapes borne along by the tide, arms waving as they tried to attract attention, to get help, to grab onto things. Others were holding onto trees, clinging on like monkeys, trying to climb out of the water. The trees looked fragile and spindly, like clumps of coral.

Ben realized their trunks were submerged: only their tops stood clear of the water.

One woman was trying to hold onto a coral-tree, but the branches wouldn't take her weight. Ben watched, appalled, as the branches snapped and she was pulled off into the current. Then he swung the binoculars away. He didn't want to see any more.

He focused on the river to the east of the ArBonCo Centre. There were more small helpless objects being swirled along. He told himself these shapes were debris, furniture, chairs from cafés; anything but people.

For miles downstream towards the obelisk of the Canary Wharf Tower, the river was lapping at windows. The roads had vanished. Ben could see cars, but they were being borne along in the water like boats, only visible as metal roofs, rocking in the current. And it was the same in the other direction.

In the windows of the buildings opposite he could see movement: rows of faces gathering to look out at the changed world. Their expressions all said the same thing:

We're trapped.

That was when it dawned on Ben that he was trapped too.

Trapped – like hundreds of thousands of Londoners, now struggling to come to terms with what had happened to them.

Struggling to survive . . .

Chapter Six

The traffic lights had been red for ages. Charleen, in her Bentley Flying Spur, sighed and put her handbrake on.

It sounded a bit odd outside. Watery.

She looked out at the traffic to either side of her. And noticed the water.

Even as she watched, the surface of the road disappeared completely. The pavements went next, engulfed by mud-coloured water. And then her whole car just seemed to die. The light behind the LCD control panel went dark, the air conditioning fell silent and the almost inaudible throb of the engine, silent as a heartbeat, was still.

£115,000-worth of Bentley never stalled. It was simply impossible. Charleen cursed and turned the key, waiting for the familiar muted roar under the bonnet which always set butterflies dancing in her stomach.

The engine turned over once and died. She turned the key back sharply and then pulled it out. Something was very wrong. The water must be so deep it had been sucked into the engine. And now she could hear a ghostly, ominous noise . . .

The roar suddenly grew louder. A muddy avalanche of water and rubbish was rumbling towards her down the road. In seconds, it was up to the doors. All around her, the cars were reduced to windowed pods poking out above the dirty swirling water.

Forget the car, she decided, panicking. She had to get out. She released the locks and pressed down the door handle.

The door wouldn't open.

She tried again, pushing her shoulder hard against it.

Nothing. The weight of the water outside was holding the door shut. The water was still rising, lapping at the windows like dirty grey lips.

A black car was coming towards her now, rocking on the water. Inside she could see the driver hammering at the windows, trying to get out. Under the water the car smashed into her bonnet with a dull crunch. Then her front wheels reared up off the ground, as if a giant hand was lifting the car.

The heavy Bentley slid along the road sideways, into a mini-van, crumpling it around a lamppost like a tin can. Two pale arms flailed against the bonnet, then slid beneath the surface of the water.

Charleen's stomach turned over. That had been the driver. She thanked heavens the Bentley was so solid. At least when it eventually stopped she'd be all right.

Then she saw the window coming up: a glossy expanse of plate glass, the lighted interior showing the foyer of a big office building. She ducked.

The plate-glass window shattered as two and a half tonnes of car hit it. The noise was amazing, high and tinkling in the watery air. Shards of glass rained down on the roof.

The arch at the top of the window smashed into the side of the car, rolling it over. Charleen found herself squashed against the ceiling, her head muzzy with the impact. The car was upside down.

And it was still moving. Outside, a confusion of shapes hurtled towards her in the murky water: a desk, chairs, printers, paper, the black eye of a computer screen. All mixed up together, as if caught in a hurricane.

Charleen started to scream . . .

Jackie got off the Northern Line at Elephant and Castle Underground Station, and made her way towards the Bakerloo Line. It was an old, dirty station and she always tried to tune out her surroundings when she used it. All she was thinking about was getting down to the Bakerloo Line so that she could continue reading the next bit of her magazine.

She walked past the heavy blast doors in the corridor, looking at her feet as she went along, careful not to step on the curved steel tracks near the doors as her stiletto heels would probably slip on them.

Why did those tracks always look so bright and shiny, as though the doors were constantly swinging to and fro over them? If you looked at the blast doors, they were thick with dust and grease. They looked like they had never moved in years – as firmly stuck in position as the riveted sections of the tunnel above.

Jackie reached the steps to the Bakerloo Line and turned to go down. She unfolded her magazine, finding her place. Nearly at the platform now.

A noise behind her made her look round. The other people in the tunnel turned back too.

The giant riveted blast doors were starting to move. For a moment Jackie thought she was hallucinating; she stopped and stared. As she watched, the door swung smoothly away from the wall to close off the passageway.

It was like someone had started a race. One moment the corridor looked quite empty: only a few people were walking to and from the platforms. The next minute they were all running towards the doors and suddenly the corridor seemed very crowded. A big guy pulled Jackie aside and pushed his way in front of her. An elderly man and his granddaughter were crushed against the wall, but no one noticed.

Everyone had just one goal: to reach those doors before they closed.

Jackie didn't see how many people got through. She was short, even in her high heels. The taller, stronger ones reached the doors before her and by the time the weight of the crowd had carried her there, the doorway was sealed shut.

She was thrown against it by the weight of the people behind her. They screamed and started to claw at the doors with their fingers, as though they could pull them open again. But they were solid steel and blast proof. Immoveable.

All over the Tube system, giant doors were closing. The network was sealing itself up.

For a moment Jackie began to wonder if she was having a peculiar dream. In a moment she would wake, either at home in bed or sitting safely on a train, her dream inspired by the sight of those heavy-duty doors and the bright steel runners in the floor. Surely she couldn't really be here, wedged against the steel doors, the ridges pushing into her ribs, forcing the air out of her lungs so that she could hardly breathe . . .

* * *

Sanjay was on a crowded Tube train, lost in the world of his iPod. The train shuddered to a halt. Even then he didn't take too much notice. It happened all the time. The train would start again soon.

The faces around him looked irritated. The people who were standing up recovered their balance, adjusted their grip on whatever rail or strap they were holding onto, and resumed what they were doing to pass the time. Some were reading novels, some newspapers; some were counting the stops on the tube map above the head of the person opposite. It was just a normal day travelling on the Tube.

Then the lights went down. That was really annoying. Sanjay took one headphone out in case there was an announcement from the driver. All he heard was people around him complaining.

'More power cuts.'

'Because of that bloody rain.'

'The other day those people were stuck in a train for two hours.'

'Two hours?!'

There was no announcement. Sanjay put the headphone back in his ear. Lemon Jelly carried on playing their cheerful electronic burbles. And on. And on.

If they *were* here for two hours, Sanjay had more than enough chillout music to stay the course.

He sat back, so relaxed he felt he could almost go to sleep. Actually it was rather pleasant being in total darkness. Because he couldn't see the faces around him, he could be anywhere.

Another track finished and Sanjay was aware of a faint squawking outside the world of his headphones. Maybe the driver was making an announcement. He took one headphone out again.

It wasn't the driver on the tannoy.

It was the sound of people screaming.

Then Sanjay realized that his legs were wet . . .

Chapter Seven

Francisco Gomez had been lying back on his concrete bunk. The mattress in the police cell was thin and provided hardly any padding. He was looking at the pattern made by the painted bricks on the opposite wall. He had been looking at it for so long that he had lost track of time.

He was thinking that he would have to get used to amusing himself like this. He doubted whether there would be any more inspiring ways of passing the time once he got to prison.

It probably wouldn't be a prison here in England. He'd been hiding out in London with his partner, but they'd almost certainly ship them back home. They were wanted in Spain for planting a car bomb in Madrid in 2001 that injured 65 people. He and his partner José Xavier had been caught in Chelsea this morning; he'd been thrown into this cell while José had been taken to another police station – he didn't know where. He wondered if José would manage to escape and reach their rendezvous.

The water came slowly. It seeped in under the door while he was staring at the wall. He only noticed it when he heard a commotion outside.

Suddenly he was aware of footsteps clattering on the bare floors. People were shouting, their words echoing as if in a subway. But that wasn't unusual in police stations. They were hardly peaceful places.

He ignored it all until he heard a sound that really surprised him. Splashing. That's when he sat up.

The floor of his cell was under half a metre of water and it was rising. The police station was flooding.

He got up off his bunk and paddled across to the steel door. He looked through the tiny hole and saw that the water was higher outside – halfway up the green-painted line that ran at waist height down the corridor. His cell was at the end – had they forgotten he was here?

He shouted out, but several black-uniformed figures were already running down the corridor towards him. They tried to open the cell door next to his, but seemed to be having problems getting in. Finally there was a rush as the water spilled gratefully in.

Francisco shouted out again. 'Hey! I thought you were looking forward to sending me home.'

Two policemen appeared at his door. 'Get back, Gomez.'

Francisco waded backwards, unsteady on his feet. 'Hurry up,' he said.

The door was unlocked. The policemen tried to pull it open, but once again the weight of water on the outside held it shut.

'Gomez, you'll have to push.' Their voices sounded worried, urgent, as if this was a matter of life and death.

He put all his weight against the door. On the other side the two officers pulled.

Something was very wrong, thought Francisco.

The door opened a crack and that was enough: the water began to pour in. With the pressure equalized the door moved open more easily.

Something else registered in Francisco's brain. Only two officers had come to get him. Normally he never had fewer than four guards.

'I thought you'd forgotten me,' said Francisco.

'We wouldn't forget you, Gomez.'

He saw they had cuffs, and felt a tiny prick of disappointment. He'd hoped they'd forgotten. One of the officers grabbed his wrists and snapped the cuffs on.

Curiously that made Francisco feel better. Usually they asked very politely if they could put handcuffs on him. Moreover, they hadn't made him turn round to cuff him behind his back. They were not bothering to do everything strictly by the book. The emergency had taken them by surprise and they had no time for their usual precautions.

How many more important details were they going to miss?

One officer linked his arm through Francisco's pinioned one. 'Get a move on, Gomez.'

The water was up to their knees now and still rising. They started to run. Their shouts echoed noisily off the brick walls, as if they were in a public swimming pool. Other officers were already on the stairs, hurrying more prisoners to the upper levels.

By the time Francisco and his escort reached the stairs, the water was up to their waists.

Francisco rushed like everyone else, but inside, mentally, he was taking his time. This emergency – whatever it was – had taken the station by surprise. They were taking shortcuts. And one of those short-cuts might be his way out.

Another of the prisoners was demanding to know what was going on. 'Where are we being taken?' His voice sounded slurred, as if he was drunk or on drugs. He had an officer on each side of him, holding him up. The guy could barely walk.

Francisco decided that might be useful. He'd try to make sure he stuck close to him.

As they climbed the stairs, the water rushed down towards them. It was dirty and smelled of mud and oil and salt. Behind them, the basement was now submerged.

The drunk in front fell over again, swearing. The concrete steps were getting slippery. Francisco nearly stumbled into him and one of his guards half hauled him up. They had reached the ground floor now, but they were still wading.

The duty officer was still sitting behind the desk, water lapping around his shins. 'Take them up to the assembly point on the roof,' he called.

Now they were on the main staircase that led to the upper floors of the station. This area was office space; it wasn't meant to house prisoners and the security was much less stringent here. Up the staircase there were big old-fashioned steel-framed windows that opened at the bottom like big cat flaps. It was hot, like a greenhouse, and one of the windows had been opened a little way.

It probably never occurred to them that it was careless. They'd probably never considered they might be escorting a terrorist up this way. These stairs were strictly for well-behaved, law-abiding staff.

Francisco saw his chance. He stuck his foot out, and the drunk crashed to the ground, pulling over the policeman who was trying to drag him up the stairs.

At the same moment Francisco brought his elbow up and struck one of his guards in the face. The officer cried out and his hand loosened its grip on Francisco's arm.

Francisco had his next move planned. He dropped to the ground and rolled over to the window. He pushed it further open with his shoulder and fell into empty space.

He landed in water and immediately went under. He tried to swim but the handcuffs were pinning his arms together. His legs cycled furiously, trying to find solid ground to push up against. He surfaced and shook the water from his eyes.

He was in a residential road in Chelsea, and it was bedlam. The water was nearly up to his waist, and in the middle of the street, cars and dustbins were being swirled along like canoes. He could hear screams and shouts.

It took him moments to suss out the best next step. He spotted a park bench heading towards him, rolled onto it and went with the flow.

Chapter Eight

For a moment, as he continued to stare through the window, Ben had almost forgotten the radio was playing in his headphones. The music seemed to belong to another world, not this strange, flooded landscape he was looking out at.

He retuned to Capital Radio for more news.

'*We're just receiving reports that central London has been flooded*,' said the DJ. His normally cheerful voice had changed completely. He sounded shocked. '*There's been an accident at the Thames Barrier and it's not functioning – London was left vulnerable to the high rainfall combined with a surge tide . . .*' He sounded confused, but the basic facts were clear. London was flooded. *'Here's Meena Chohan, our traffic reporter, up in the Flying Eye,'* he finished.

The sound of a light aircraft engine came on in the background, and Ben heard the voice of the female reporter who had been speaking earlier.

'I'm over East London right now and the scene is unbelievable. The river is as wide as a lake. The runways of City Airport have disappeared. Docklands has disappeared. The Docklands Light Railway has vanished. Central London and the City are just a mass of towers sticking up out of the water.' Her voice sounded shaky, disbelieving, appalled . . .

'The flooding just goes on and on. Usually when we're up here doing traffic reports, we navigate by the pattern of roads and roundabouts. They have all gone.'

Ben caught a glimpse of a small blue object, moving across the sky on the east side of the building. He ran round to watch it. That was Capital Radio's plane, the Flying Eye.

'It looks like a completely different city,' Meena Chohan continued. *'That water's got to be at least*

three metres deep. There's some dry land up where it's higher. St Paul's is OK, but there's water lapping at the bottom steps. The devastation is incredible. I've never seen anything like it.'

Ben started to walk around the perimeter of the gallery. The building was completely surrounded by water. Water that was moving, carrying along cars, street furniture and helpless people. He was still carrying the binoculars and he lifted them to his eyes to look more closely. He remembered the helpless people he had seen grabbing at lampposts, trees – anything. Helpless as ants. It reminded him of some of the footage he had seen on the TV of the Asian tsunami. He put the binoculars down again.

He supposed Cally would come for him soon. Then he had a horrible thought. Where was she? She'd gone down to the conference room in the basement.

Had she got out?

Would she have had time? The basement was three flights down from the ground floor and the water had flooded in so rapidly.

Could his mother's friend be dead?

'*Regent Street seems to be dry,*' said Meena

Chohan, '*but there are people and traffic everywhere. It's chaos. Buckingham Palace has escaped for the moment but the Mall's under water. Most of Westminster's cut off.*'

Westminster. That was where his mum was.

Ben ran round to the front of the building again. The terraces of Westminster had gone. The water lapped at the windows so that the Houses of Parliament looked like a famous painting he had seen of Venice. Where was Bel having her meeting?

He got out his phone and speed-dialled her number. *I don't care if you're in a meeting*, he said to himself. *For once, just answer.*

He didn't expect her to answer, of course. He expected her abrasive answerphone message again but he never even got a ring tone. Instead he got an automated message from the phone company. '*Lines are busy. Please try—*'

The message was cut off. There was silence. He tried again but there was nothing – not even the message that told him her phone was out of reach.

He tried home; his dad in Macclesfield.

Nothing. It was as if the battery was dead. But it

wasn't: the display was glowing as usual and the battery icon showed more than half charged. But the signal display was blank.

A bang like a firework going off made Ben look out of the window again. At the same moment the lights in the gallery went out. He saw that the lights in all the buildings nearby were down. There had been a massive power cut.

The London Eye had stopped. At the bottom, glowing sparks were fizzing out of the mechanism. Ben watched as two parents, up to their waists in water in a half-submerged capsule, struggled to lift their three young children onto their shoulders. The official escort in the navy London Eye uniform was frantically searching for a window that opened.

Further up, other passengers started to notice the panicking passengers below. They hammered on the glass with cameras and shoes, until the whole wheel looked like a grotesque mobile, a painting of hell, the pods swinging as people tried to escape from their glass prisons.

The glass in one of the higher pods sprayed out in a shower. A figure in a red cagoule hurtled out into the air – feet first, nose held as if anticipating the plunge into the water. Another followed, legs and arms cycling in the air as if he had lost control of them. The figure in the red cagoule hit the water. The other figure splashed down soon after.

Slowly Ben raised the binoculars and watched.

The jumpers had underestimated the fierce current. He saw flailing arms rise briefly above the choppy surface, already being carried away from the Eye like twigs caught in a whirlpool. Once again, he lowered the binoculars, but he could still see the small helpless figures. They were swept towards the concrete walls of the ArBonCo Centre. He didn't see them hit, but he did see the tide suck them away again. When it did they were unmoving, lifeless.

Ben felt sick. He put the binoculars down on the window ledge and turned away.

Strange – if he looked at the room, it was as if nothing had happened. Outside the windows, the sky was the same grey as it had been before. The carpets, the easy chairs, the low tables all looked so everyday. The only thing that was odd was that all the lights had gone out.

What should he do? Hide up here? It seemed nice and safe and normal.

And then the creeping fear began to steal up on Ben as well. He began to notice the sounds. No, it was not normal. Car and burglar alarms shrieked from the streets below. And there was another sound: muffled shouts and screams. Once he became aware of them, Ben couldn't block them out. They filled him with fear, just as the people in the London Eye had transmitted their panic to each other, reverberating through the spokes of that giant wheel.

He didn't want to stay here alone.

Chapter Nine

In the middle of the gallery was a green EXIT sign and a pair of fire doors.

Ben ran for them. He snatched the doors open and started to run down the white marble-tiled stairwell. Somewhere below him, he heard running footsteps – so many that it was like distant machine-gun fire. And shouting and screaming, louder now. He went down past one door, then another, then another. Floor after floor went by. The sounds grew louder. Ben kept his hand on the black handrail, counting down the floors, swinging round and round as he went. Floor five . . . four . . . three.

He caught up with a small group of people, who barely looked at him, all intent on getting out. They were half jogging down the stairs, not daring to run fast but too frightened to walk.

When they reached the second floor, they saw a man wearing a red armband printed with the words FIRE MARSHAL. He was waving people in through the open fire door, like a policeman directing traffic.

Ben caught a glimpse of something further down the stairwell. Something black, glossy and moving. The building was full of water. He wondered with a sinking feeling in the pit of his stomach whether Cally was still down there.

'In here, please,' said the fire marshal, and Ben obeyed.

It was a big, open-plan room, which took up nearly the entire floor of the building. It was full of people sitting in chairs, on desks, leaning against the window ledges. They looked calm and orderly, all waiting patiently. The ones who had just arrived were joining a queue and filing past another fire marshal, who was ticking off names on a list.

Ben joined the queue. He felt better now that he

was with people, reassured by the queues. OK, he thought. Maybe we'll all be all right. But there was a smell in the room: cold sweat and fear.

There was another smell too – something salty, tarry. And a sound, like gentle splashing. The water was lapping just below the windows.

It was Ben's turn to be checked on the register. Another fire marshal peered at him. 'Who are you?' His list of personnel ran to several pages. The building must have thousands of people working in it.

'I'm a visitor,' said Ben.

'Who were you with?'

'Cally—' Ben realized he didn't know her surname. 'Cally in Clean Fuels Research.' He looked around the room, hoping to catch sight of her.

The pen scanned up and down the list, over the page, found a name and hovered. 'Is she with you?'

Ben hesitated. 'No.'

'Where is she? She shouldn't have left you alone. Visitors shouldn't be unaccompanied. Where is she?'

Ben didn't want to say. His throat was dry. It took him a few goes to get the words out. 'She went to a meeting in the basement.'

71

The fire marshal didn't look up. He kept his pen over Cally's name for a moment, then put a dot in the margin next to it. Ben stared at it.

Then the man waved him on.

A woman sitting at a desk beckoned Ben over. Beside her was a big green first aid kit; a man in glasses was dabbing antiseptic on a gash in his arm. 'Have you got any injuries?' she asked Ben.

He shook his head. 'No. I'm fine.'

'OK. Find a seat and wait for instructions.'

Ben did as he was told. He approached a group of people who were sitting chatting. They looked almost unconcerned, though he noticed that one had a bruise over one eye. Most of them had rucksacks or bags with them, and coats. He passed some people who must have escaped from the flood water outside too – a woman was rubbing her legs with a towel; her companions' jeans were wet up to the knees; high-heeled boots lay discarded on the floor, the leather soaked through. It grew darker as Ben made his way towards the middle of the floor, away from the windows. He could see tiny patches of light as people used their mobiles as torches to read, or listened to music or played games.

A slim woman with her hair covered in a headscarf spotted Ben. 'What's happening?' she asked.

'I don't know,' said Ben.

A plump woman in a long skirt, wet up to the knees, answered her. 'The police said to stay here and we'd be evacuated.'

Ben leaned on the window ledge and looked across to the Houses of Parliament. Now that he wasn't so high up, the river looked even more vast. A plume of sparks rose into the sky like fireworks. What was it – an electricity substation shorting out? He got out his phone again. The display said there was no signal.

'You won't get anything on that,' said a voice.

A balding man in a light grey suit was watching Ben morosely. There was something smug about the way he said it, as if he was enjoying Ben's disappointment.

'No harm in trying,' said Ben cheerily.

The balding man looked taken aback and moved on. Ben was suddenly reminded of the louts he'd met on the train, seeing what they could do to upset the other passengers. Perhaps one day the pierced bullies might be wearing suits and going bald. That made him smile.

He looked out of the window again. Big Ben said ten to two; his watch said two fifteen. Then he knew the world really *had* gone wrong: Big Ben had stopped.

A loud bang and a flash shattered the hushed conversations. Ben, along with all the people at that end of the floor, found himself instinctively pushing away from the explosion. All around him he heard screams.

After a few moments everyone stopped and looked back, like wild animals that had been spooked. A cupboard was belching thick smoke into the room. Sparks of orange-yellow and blue light showed behind the door.

Then the chaos started. Everyone began to talk at once. 'The sprinklers will come on in a minute.'

'They won't. They'll have shorted too.'

The light show continued behind the cupboard door. 'All the electrics are on fire in there.'

Then Ben noticed that one of the windows was

open; a thin man in a dark, sweat-stained shirt was sitting on the window ledge, looking down at the water lapping at the white marble building just a couple of metres below.

Ben remembered the helpless figures hurled by the tide against the concrete walls outside. He pushed through the group of people and seized the man's arm.

'Don't,' he said.

The man looked at him angrily. 'I'm a strong swimmer – I can get to that rail bridge over there.'

Ben kept his voice calm and looked into the man's eyes. 'I just saw someone die doing that. They must have thought they could make it too. The current is too strong.'

The man's colleagues were obviously also having doubts. 'Don't, Richard,' said the woman with the wet gypsy skirt. 'There must be another way.'

Richard sighed, then got to his feet, turned and carefully lowered himself back into the room.

Suddenly the door of the burning cupboard burst open and smacked against the wall. Smoke billowed out, along with a smell of burning cable. From the floor above there was another bang.

As the crowd surged away from the fire, Ben gradually found himself swept to one side. His elbow caught a door handle and he stumbled backwards into an adjoining room – a small meeting room.

The stinking cloud of smoke followed him in . . .

Chapter Ten

Ben realized that there were three other people with him in the room: sweaty-shirted Richard; a young Chinese man with an identity pass on his belt that said his name was Guang and he worked in the IT department; and a woman in a glittery top. They stared at the smoke filling the room outside, listened to the screams and the sounds of running feet.

'It's the transformer for this floor,' Guang said. 'It must have shorted. That smoke will be nasty.'

On the other side of the room's glass wall was a frosted transfer with the ArBonCo logo. It began to blur as the heat melted it. A figure appeared through the smoke and Ben recognized the thin woman in the headscarf he had spoken to earlier. The woman in the glittery top let her in. She came in coughing on a wave of heat, as though she had escaped from an oven.

'Cheryl, bring her over here to get some air.' Guang edged around the big table in the middle of the room and opened the windows onto the river. The new arrival leaned on the table, coughing. Cheryl, the woman in the glittery top, put her arms around her shoulders and led her to the window. 'Come on, Kabeera. You'll feel better in a minute.'

Ben noticed that the smoke outside was getting thicker. Richard was standing glaring at him. 'You stopped me getting out. I'd have swum to that bridge by now,' he told him.

No you wouldn't, thought Ben, but if I say so we'll just have a pointless argument. On the wall was a display of rescue equipment for oil rigs, including a big, orange inflatable raft.

'Maybe we don't have to swim,' said Ben. He moved quickly to the wall and pulled the raft down. 'Help me with this.'

Richard looked at him mutinously, refusing to help.

Ben realized that he couldn't waste time trying to talk him round. If Bel had been here, she'd have told him he was being an idiot. He'd get the others involved instead. What were their names? Ben searched his brain. Oh, yes. 'Guang, Kabeera – we've got a raft!' Ben tugged the raft off the wall and laid it on the conference table in the middle of the room.

Cheryl grabbed the other two, and pointed at the raft on the table. 'Quick, help with this.'

'Where do we inflate it?' Guang asked. 'Everybody look for a valve or a gas canister.'

On the other side of the glass, the smoke was thick and grey, like insulating wool. All the plastic frosting had turned black and charred. Everyone patted the orange material, searching for the inflation valve. They didn't have much time.

Richard found it. 'It's here,' he called. 'And there's no gas canister. So what do we do, blow it up like a balloon?'

It was true. Where there would usually be a tube of compressed gas to inflate the raft, there was just a tab of black fabric. Richard glared at Ben, as though this was all his fault. He really is a sore loser, he thought.

Suddenly, behind them, there was a bang. Cheryl screamed and Kabeera jumped. A jagged spar of glass the height of the door crashed down into the table between Ben and Richard. It smashed into shards like daggers. They stood frozen, shaken. Ben slowly looked round.

The glass door had cracked from top to bottom. The door handle was metal and it must have expanded, sending stresses through the glass. Hot smoke began to billow through the hole.

Kabeera was yelling but the smoke caught her throat and she started coughing again. Cheryl looked at her and suddenly understood what she was trying to say. 'Use the fire extinguisher!' she yelled. 'Blow it up using the fire extinguisher!'

All at once they were acting together, like a team. Ben pulled the fire extinguisher off the wall. Richard smoothed down the fabric of the raft so that Guang could locate the valve again. Kabeera was coughing, but she and Cheryl managed to push the window open wide.

Ben put the nozzle of the fire extinguisher up against the valve and pulled the trigger. There was a hiss as the foam flowed into the material. The raft began to take shape – then stopped.

Ben pressed the trigger again, but the extinguisher was empty. And the raft was only half inflated.

The temperature was rising and the hot smoke was starting to fill the room.

There wasn't another fire extinguisher; and anyway, there was no time to use it. Guang's voice rang out. '*Let's go!*'

Cheryl and Kabeera helped to drag the raft into place on the sill. The smoke curled out of the window, making dark clouds in the wet air. Richard dragged a chair across the carpet to act as a mounting block. Kabeera pulled her headscarf up a little higher to try and protect her throat, but she was still coughing as she climbed up.

One by one they scrambled onto the raft. Kabeera and Cheryl each went to the front and hung onto the ropes. Ben climbed out and inched his way across. The raft felt soft, like a lilo feels when it is going down. Would it hold? As he looked down he saw the water surging less than a metre below, smashing a wooden chair against the white walls. He remembered those people who had jumped from the London Eye, just bags of bones in the tide by now.

He must have frozen where he was on the sill. Guang tapped him on the shoulder and pointed. 'You go over there and hang onto that rope in the middle.'

Ben had little choice. Water was better than fire.

Guang and Richard held on at the back, then they pushed away from the window frame. The raft slid easily on the wet windowsill. For a moment it was airborne, then it plunged into the water.

Chapter Eleven

Ben clung on. Filthy Thames water sluiced over his head. The water was icy cold, sending pains all over his body and making his fingers go numb instantly. His brain played him terrifying images – the woman struggling to climb the coral-tree while the water battered its branches like an angry demon trying to shake her loose.

Freezing spray filled his eyes, nose and mouth. It tasted of mud and oil. They were travelling fast, as if on rapids, completely at the mercy of the current. The raft wobbled and undulated under them, as though it was about to fold in half at any moment. Ben could make out shapes crouched against the other end, but the spray kept forcing his eyes closed. The only things he could see with any certainty were right beside him in the water, buffeted against the raft: a blackboard sign from a pub; litter bins, surrounded by a confetti of KFC wrappers, coffee cups, tickets, leaflets, half-eaten burgers. A small bundle of drenched clothes bobbed up nearby. Ben saw a face, wet hair like streaks of black seaweed dragged across the forehead. A body. He couldn't tell if it was male or female. Then it was swept away from them again.

Suddenly Ben spotted a short black spike in the water. He realized it was the top of a lamppost and his brain did a quick reality check. Those lampposts on the South Bank were about three metres high. He got a sudden blinding sense of panic at the thought of all the water below him. And what if something tore the raft?

Still the current pulled them on. They passed a man helplessly riding a giant seesaw in the air above them. He was clinging onto the gangplank of a restaurant boat, which was waving free over the water. His face was grim, unseeing.

Now they were passing Westminster Bridge, gliding over the approach road. The bridge itself had shrunk to a small hump in the middle of the water, and Ben could see boats and a floating restaurant stuck at the arch, thumping against the concrete as though the current was trying to use them as a battering ram to smash through to the other side. To their left a Day-Glo orange van hurtled towards a tall grey building and crashed in through one of the windows, leaving a black hole. Ben's heart turned a somersault. Suppose they were carried into a building? Into the dark? Into a fire?

Suddenly he realized that one of the shapes on the raft had gone. He looked at the empty section of rope. Just like that, without a sound, one of the people who had been in that room had disappeared. One minute they were there, the next they were gone. Who was it? Ben couldn't recognize any of the remaining shapes. They were all soaking wet, their clothes darkened by the water, their hair plastered down. Just lumps of wet clothes. He looked around in the water, searching for someone in trouble.

A big powerboat came speeding past, as tall as a

two-storey building. It clipped the raft and sent it whirling round like a fairground ride. Ben hung on, blinded by spray. The raft bounced off a double-decker bus, a truck, a park bench, a bin, all the time undulating like a waterbed. It felt loose, as though it was about to deflate entirely and leave them all struggling in the waves like debris. He was so cold, but he had to stay still and cling on. He felt like he was only a set of fingers clamped around a piece of rope, waiting for it all to stop. The rope was digging into his hands. Everything hurt.

They glided on past the Houses of Parliament, strangely stunted now that their lower floors were submerged. The graceful tower of Big Ben stood above it all, aloof from the chaos. Beyond it Ben could see what looked like a battleship nudging at the gothic windows of Westminster Abbey. All at once he recognized it as HMS *Belfast*, which he'd been to see on a previous trip with his mother. It had drifted off its moorings on the other side of the river. It was a surreal sight, these two pieces of London history juxtaposed like that. If I'm going to die, he thought, let it be now. With that image in my head.

They circled past the abbey and then on down a street of tall white buildings. Ben's mind was replaying the image of the van disappearing through the window, but they were swept on past the buildings and into an open area.

Here, only the tops of trees were poking up out of the water. They must be floating across one of the parks. That was even more frightening – it was like drifting out at sea.

Suddenly the raft hit a tree and Ben was slithering into the water. The raft was bobbing away from him. The last thing he saw was its orange sides, now with only three hunched figures clinging on, unaware they were leaving one more behind.

Chapter Twelve

Ben disappeared under the water. He surfaced spluttering, his mouth full of foul-tasting water. He imagined lampposts and trees below him, which meant the water was really deep here. His arms and legs flailed about, trying to find something to cling to. Anything to avoid being swept along by the current like another piece of flotsam.

A big shape surged past. He didn't know what it was but something made him pull himself towards it in a strong front crawl. The current held him back as though it had anchored his feet.

No, thought Ben. *I'm not giving up.* He put every

ounce of his remaining strength into swimming towards whatever it was. As he approached it, he could make out red metallic paint . . . a chrome bar. It was the top of a car with a roof rack.

That gave him the extra focus he needed. He looked at the bright metal roof rack and imagined his hands grasping it. Just a few more strokes and he would have something to hold onto again. The effort was agonizing, but still he pulled himself forward. Slowly the bar came closer. He reached out and his fingers brushed against it. Nearly. But then he felt the current threatening to sweep him away. He grabbed at the roof rack like a man trying to catch a trapeze bar.

Then he felt solid metal under his fingers. He'd done it. He took hold with his other hand and pulled himself forward, hand over hand. Only when he felt something solid under his body did he stop.

That's it, he thought, and closed his eyes. Now I can let the water take me where it wants again.

After a few moments he looked around. The water was becoming shallower. Now he could see more of the roof of the car. Ahead there were more buildings, grand-looking, covered in white stucco like wedding cake. And the dark shiny surface of wet tarmac. He'd reached the edge of the flooded area.

Ben rolled off the car and into the water. It was up to his waist and he struggled to keep his feet. But he fixed his eyes on those white wedding-cake buildings and half ran, half swam towards them.

Finally he reached dry land and collapsed gratefully onto the tarmac. He had never felt so exhausted in his life.

A six-seater twin-engined Piper Seneca in dark blue livery with white logos glided across the sky. One thousand feet up and doing a hundred and thirty knots, the Flying Eye was cruising much lower than passenger jets. That was the first thing that Meena Chohan had noticed when she had taken over as Capital Radio's traffic reporter. If you came into London on a passenger jet, the city looked like a charming toy, jewelled with lights. If you came in on the Flying Eye you saw a bigger, grubbier London.

Today, looking out over the city was a shock all over again. Meena had never seen anything so forbidding. The sky was the colour of dark dishwater. The flooded area was an inky slick through the familiar city. Not one light shone. When the water poured in, it had extinguished all the office lights, traffic lights, car lights and shop signs, and left everything in darkness. There weren't even any orange and blue flashing lights from emergency vehicles.

The darkness had even leaked out to the dry areas. But here at least there were cars: red brake lights and bright headlights trying to escape the capital on gridlocked roads. It was a ghostly sight.

Meena unbuckled her seatbelt and reached behind her. She unzipped her bag and pulled her phone out, then put it up to her eye.

Mike Rogers, the pilot, looked at her disbelievingly. 'What are you doing?'

'Take us down closer.'

'Are you mad? We should be getting back.'

Meena had started her career as a journalist on a local paper. She had hung around outside hospitals, court rooms and pubs, alert for the tiny event that would turn into the big story, the scoop that she could sell to the nationals. Old habits died hard. She turned and gave Mike her most pleading look with her deep brown eyes. 'Please, Mike. Nobody else will get pictures like this. It's a historic moment.'

'They're not going to come out anyway, taken with a phone.'

Meena had the viewfinder to her eye as she leaned out of the open window into the rain. 'This isn't just a phone with a poxy camera. It's a kick-ass camera with eight megapixels and four times zoom. And anyway, it doesn't matter if the quality's a bit rubbish if the subject matter's unique.'

'Meena,' said Mike, 'air traffic control is out. We can't go flying around wherever we please. We need to maintain our height and go back.'

Meena wasn't going to be put off. 'There's no one else out here. Who are we going to crash into?'

If Mike answered, she didn't hear it.

'Oh my God,' she said. 'Look at Westminster. Come on, don't be a spoilsport. Just a bit closer.'

As Mike took the plane down, Meena saw plenty to snap. Sinking vehicles collided with boats, all coated with the muddy river water. Smoke curled out of buildings, sometimes accompanied by the orange glow of flames. There were people trying to get to dry land on whatever they could find. She saw three people on an orange raft and snapped that. Others remained in their buildings, looking out of the windows at the devastation and wondering what to do.

The bridges down the Thames were just small humps, crowded with stranded people. The high-level railway bridge that led into Waterloo was a thin line with a train standing on top. People lined its length like birds on a telephone cable. At the water's edge people were crawling out amidst dead bodies and rubbish.

'Take us over Leicester Square,' she said.

Mike obliged and took the plane in a circle.

Leicester Square was where Capital's studios were. Neither of them had heard from the radio station for a good fifteen minutes now. Normally they had it playing softly in the background, and Meena listened in with one ear so that she was ready for her bulletins. Although she received cues from the producer through an earpiece, it helped to listen to the show. It didn't look good if there had been a running joke about getting up late, for instance, and the DJ brought it up and she didn't get the reference. The listeners wanted them to be one big happy bunch of friends, sharing jokes.

'What's it like?' said Mike. They were over Leicester Square now, but he was keeping his eyes on the controls.

'It's dark. Really dark. It's not flooded but there seems to be debris everywhere. Umbrellas, bags, rubbish. As though there were loads of people there and they've run away. Probably all came out of the cinemas when the power failed. Imagine being in there when the lights went out.'

'The lights are generally out in cinemas,' said Mike.

'You know what I mean,' said Meena, and took a picture.

'Bet no one's in the office,' said Mike.

'I wouldn't be so sure,' said Meena. 'I bet Jimmy's still in the newsroom. A good journalist doesn't desert his post.'

Mike made a disbelieving noise. 'They'll have gone

just like anyone else. Just like we should.' He took the plane round in a big circle towards the east, back towards the airfield in Essex.

As the plane banked Meena spotted the crowds walking up Shaftesbury Avenue. Everyone was heading away from the flood, trying to escape. Where were they going? That area of London was mainly offices or theatres or shops; nobody lived there. People were all deserting it, trying to get home.

A voice came over the intercom from air traffic control. '*Hello, Flying Eye. Are you receiving? Sorry about the interruption. We had a power cut there. Are you OK? Over.*'

Mike answered, the relief in his voice obvious. 'We're receiving you loud and clear. Over.'

Meena spoke into her mouthpiece. 'Mike, ask them if they've heard anything from the guys at the studio.'

Mike asked the question. While Meena waited for the reply, she leaned out again and took a picture as they passed over Tower Bridge. The roads around it had vanished and it looked like a forlorn remnant of London, stuck in the upright position, the two halves of its road deck protruding into the air like a broken toy.

'No, *nothing. There are power cuts everywhere. We're running on emergency generators. The National Grid's completely shorted. It's dark from Birmingham all the way to the coast. You'd better come back.*'

Meena didn't want to leave the action. 'Mike, tell them there are still a lot of people trying to get out of town on the roads. Shouldn't we stay out here to give them updates?'

Mike passed her question on. The reply was instant. '*No point. The transmitter's down. The emergency services want us to clear the airspace.*'

The Millennium Dome came up, shrunk to the size of a saucer. Meena saw that there were people standing on top, waving at the plane.

'Mike, tell them to report to the emergency services that there are people on the Dome who need to be rescued,' she said urgently.

The next thing they saw was the Thames Barrier itself – the row of silver metal humps protruding from the water. The big ship was still stranded on one of them, a cluster of small boats tethered alongside it like doctors attending a bedridden patient. Meena snapped it too. 'Wow. I've seen some traffic accidents in my time but that one's got to win the prize.'

Mike spoke to Control. 'Is there anything we can do before we come back in?'

'No. *Just be thankful and get the hell out of there.*'

Chapter Thirteen

Ben was still sitting on the pavement, his back against the wall. Rain washed down over his face, his hands, his clothes. He let it; at least it would hose off the river water.

After a while he began to look around. He was on a road with grand-looking buildings on each side.

There were pools of water everywhere, like the seashore after the tide has gone out. The water's edge was a few metres away, lapping around the buildings on the south side of the road. Seagulls wheeled overhead. Geese strutted around the puddles. They must have been carried here from the lakes in the park. A swan sat beside a wrecked car as though guarding it.

But where were all the people?

When he reached dry land, Ben had expected to find fire engines, ambulances, police officers, but he couldn't see anyone – just a few abandoned vehicles. Just across the road, a van had crashed into a taxi and a car. Their bonnets were crumpled, the doors left open. The van's windscreen had shattered and oil was leaking from underneath the taxi, giving the water an iridescent sheen.

Only the wail of burglar and car alarms joined the desolate cries of the seagulls. Some of the sounds came from under the water, as though the drowned vehicles were calling for help.

Ben got up and started to move. He was freezing. He stomped over to the taxi and peered in. There was nothing in it. Then he saw that the boot of the car had shot open; folded up inside, he could see a raincoat. Without even thinking he pulled it out and put it on.

It must have been expensive – a pale grey Burberry mac with a checked interior, still dry despite the rain that had been pouring into the boot. 'Sorry,' he muttered. He didn't know who he was talking to but it felt very wrong to be taking things like that. And his dirty wet top would probably leave marks on the lining. He couldn't help it, though. He desperately needed to get warm.

The next thought that came to him wiped the smile right off his face again: his wallet had fallen out of his pocket so he had no money and no ticket home. What should he do?

Even with the coat, Ben began to shiver. He felt very, very alone.

Why were there no people around? Why was no one organizing rescue parties? He wanted to find people who would know what to do. Like there had been at ArBonCo.

Like at ArBonCo. He remembered Kabeera, Cheryl, Guang and difficult Richard, his companions on the raft. He wondered where their journeys had ended – who was it who had fallen off before him, and had the other three reached dry ground?

He thought about Cally. Less than an hour ago she had been embarrassing him by telling him how he'd grown. Now she might be dead. And what about Bel . . . ?

That made him pull himself together. His journey on the raft had ended with him here, safe on dry land. Surely what happened from now on couldn't be as bad as that. *Think clearly*, he told himself. *What's the best thing to do now?*

He pulled the Burberry around him and did up the belt while he thought. Suddenly it came to him. Charing Cross. He'd arranged to meet Bel there at 3.30. Surely she would be doing everything in her power to make the appointment. And with no phones working, going to Charing Cross was the only way he could meet up with her again.

He looked at his watch. The digital display was blank – of course, it had died in the water too. Another thought came to him, stopping him in his tracks like an axe blow. Had Bel managed to get safely away from Westminster? Why had he never wondered if she might be in danger? *Would* she be at Charing Cross waiting for him? Or was she . . . ?

Immediately Ben felt a wave of anger. *You'd better have got away,* he thought. *You've already rearranged our day. I've already had to kill time while you went to your meeting with some politician. He probably*

*didn't want to talk to you anyway – they usually
don't. You'd better not leave me on my own in this
wrecked city. Charing Cross, 3.30, you said. You'd
better be there.*

Now that he had a plan he felt better. But it gave
him more problems to solve. How should he get
there? He didn't know London that well. What if
Charing Cross was underwater?

No point in thinking like that. If he found that it
was flooded, he'd work out something else to do. The
most important thing was to try to get there.

A map. He needed a map. He had no money to buy
one so he would have to borrow one again. He went
back to the car, but it seemed to be empty of anything
useful. Then he peered in through the taxi's open
door, the swan watching his every move with black,
alien eyes.

He couldn't see a map. Maybe taxi drivers didn't
need them because they knew the streets off by heart.
He reached in to open the glove compartment, but his
hand paused. It felt like stealing.

It's not stealing, he told himself. *It's survival.
I'm only looking for a map, not money or valuables*

or anything. And the taxi has been abandoned.

There was no map in there anyway. He would have to try the van.

As he walked round the front of the taxi, smashed brake and indicator lights crunched under his feet, making a wet mosaic of red and orange plastic.

Ben was keeping an eye on the swan, which was still glaring at him. He moved slowly and spoke to it soothingly. 'I only want to look for a map. I'm not going to hurt you.' He turned away to open the van door.

A honking sound behind him made him whirl round again. The swan was on its feet, half hopping, half charging towards him. Its wings were spread and its head was hooked backwards, like a cobra about to strike.

Ben had heard of swans attacking people but he'd never quite believed it. And until now he'd never realized how big they were and how fierce they looked.

The wings beat ferociously, making a noise like wind snatching at a heavy sail. Another fact he'd heard about swans popped into Ben's head.

Apparently a swan could break your leg with a blow of its wings. Rubbish, he'd thought. But he changed his mind when he heard the sound of those powerful wings.

The swan's neck uncoiled and its orange beak thrust forward like a dart. Ben backed away, fast.

The bird hopped awkwardly towards him and he retreated further, ready to run. But after another thrust with its beak the swan settled down on the ground again.

Ben stood, frozen. Was it safe to move again?

Then he saw blood trickling into the oily puddle and remembered the swan's awkward hopping gait. It was injured. That must be why it had attacked.

He continued to back away, his hands low in a gesture of apology. 'I'm sorry.'

There was another abandoned car on the other side of the road, its front crumpled into a lamppost. As Ben made his way across, a Canada goose came waddling towards him. He stopped, watching it carefully, alert to the slightest sign of aggression in the way it carried its slender black neck. But he soon realized that it wasn't interested in him. It began to root through the contents of an upturned bin.

Ben peered into the car and spotted what he wanted lying on the passenger seat: a battered A–Z of London. He opened the door and picked it up. 'Sorry,' he said to the departed owner, and closed the door again. In the last five minutes he'd been saying that word constantly.

Right, where was he? There was a sign on the building on the corner: Eaton Square. Ben opened the A–Z, but the rain was soaking through the pages. He closed it again, opened the car door and got in. It was such a relief to be out of the rain.

He found Eaton Square in the index. It was near Victoria Station and Buckingham Palace. Most importantly he wasn't too far from Charing Cross – probably a twenty-minute walk. Provided he didn't run into any more injured animals.

He looked out at the dismal sky. Having a roof over his head was such a relief. Above him, the rain drummed down relentlessly. He wondered for a moment whether to stay where he was; at least it would be dry. But the rain might continue for hours and if Bel was already at Charing Cross, she would be waiting. Worrying.

He got out, and shuddered as the rain trickled down his neck again. He muttered a warning to Bel under his breath as he started off: *You'd better be at Charing Cross when I get there.*

After a few minutes he came to a telephone box. Relief flooded through him, along with an overwhelming sense of homesickness. He didn't have to be alone: he could phone his dad.

He pushed the door open gratefully, then looked at the phone for a moment, wondering what to do. He couldn't remember the last time he'd used a call box as he usually had his mobile. This one took coins – which was no good – but it also had a number you could call to reverse the charges. Just what he needed. He picked up the receiver.

Nothing. It was dead.

Of course it was. Why had he thought it wouldn't be?

He jiggled the cradle up and down a few times, hoping the phone would come to life.

Ben started when a car horn suddenly blared out in

the empty streets. He looked around. Where had it come from? There were people out there – but where?

He couldn't see anything, but the rain was blurring the windows of the phone booth: it was like trying to see out of a shower cubicle. He put his head out but the street was empty.

Another sound made him look again. It was the roar of a car engine. Ben jumped out of the phone booth, waving madly. Headlights came speeding towards him. He waved again – perhaps he could get a lift. Just to be with other people would be good.

But the car swished past, sending up a wake of spray like a boat. Ben stared after it as it raced towards a junction, where dark traffic lights stood watching mutely. Its brake lights come on momentarily, then it wheeled round the corner and disappeared.

Ben felt disbelief, then crushing disappointment. Surely the driver must have seen him. If it had been him or his dad and they'd seen someone alone in a situation like this, they wouldn't have just left them.

But this was the big city. He remembered that girl

he'd helped with her luggage at Waterloo. Vicky James; he'd even remembered her name. Everyone else, though, had blanked her. In London, if you didn't know anyone, you were on your own.

Chapter Fourteen

But he wasn't totally alone.

As he made his way to the junction, he caught a glimpse of movement at an upper-storey window. Someone was watching him.

'Hello?' he called, and waved.

The movement stopped. The figure had moved away from the window, not wanting to be seen.

In another house Ben could see a shadowy figure behind a large frosted window. Someone was hurrying up a flight of stairs, a box in his arms.

'Hello?!' he shouted.

The shadow quickened its pace up the stairs and vanished, as if it was afraid of him.

At the junction Ben picked a turning and found himself in a road with a few shops – a newsagent and a delicatessen.

The delicatessen was dark, but in the window, arranged on a marble slab, there were loaves of bread and delicious-looking savoury pastries. Ben's stomach rumbled at the sight of them. He must have used up a lot of calories keeping warm in the water. He tried the door but it was locked.

Reluctantly he tore himself away and trudged on, turning off into another street. The first buildings he came to were hotels. Their names were picked out in neon letters over the doors, but the signs were dark.

A big four-by-four in a parking bay started to shriek, its indicators flashing. The noise continued for about thirty seconds and then stopped. Ben couldn't see what could have set it off and no one came to investigate. Other alarms and sirens sounded in the distance, as if in answer. Thirty seconds later the alarm came on again. How long would it carry on like that? Until its battery was dead?

Was there another sound too, mingling with the far-off sounds of alarms and sirens. Human cries?

Or was that his imagination?

Down a side street Ben caught sight of a figure trudging slowly along, head bent against the rain. The man was walking away from him, but Ben's heart leaped at the thought of company. Should he run to join him? This trek was so lonely. He had never had to fend for himself and make all these decisions before. He yearned to have someone to talk to, the reassurance of another human being. Someone to stop him imagining he heard screams in the wail of a car alarm.

No, Ben told himself. *I know where I'm going. Keep to the plan.*

As he walked on, he caught sight of himself in the window of a bookshop. He looked bedraggled, as if he'd been sleeping rough. The expensive Burberry mac on top of his sodden jeans was obviously stolen. No wonder no one wanted to stop for him; he looked a real vagabond.

He glanced down a flooded street and saw a red dinghy with an outboard motor chugging slowly along between the buildings, at first-floor level. One of the boat's three occupants was standing up, looking in through the windows. They were dressed for the weather in heavy-duty rubberized yellow sailing coats.

They must be looking for people in trouble, thought Ben. At least some people were helping each other. It restored his faith in human nature.

In a richly furnished house down one of the flooded streets, a middle-aged couple were carrying boxes up the stairs.

'There's a boat out there,' said the woman, spotting the small dinghy chugging along outside the window. She came into the living room and put the box down on a black bin liner on the pale carpet. It contained their passports, building society books and share certificates from the safe downstairs. Another box was filled with the jewellery she had inherited from her grandmother – a diamond necklace and a string of pearls. They lay in satin-lined leather boxes on top of some other essentials – some bottles of water, a few croissants and the keys to the BMW in the garage – although the car was probably ruined: the garage was in the basement and the whole ground floor was underwater.

Those boxes were all the couple had been able to salvage from the ground floor when the flood started.

'Did you hear me?' said the woman. 'I said there's a boat out there. People are getting out of London . . . Do you think we ought to?'

Her husband was easing his wellington boots off, careful to keep them on a black bin liner so that he didn't mark the carpet. 'No, we should be all right here.'

The woman noticed that one of the men outside was standing up in the boat. She waved at him and he waved back. The boat stopped beside the window to the stairwell, so she put down her box, crossed to the window and opened it to talk to them.

Two of the men climbed in without waiting to be invited, muddy water dripping off their boots.

The owners were a bit surprised, but then it all turned very strange indeed. For, shockingly, unbelievably, rather than helping them, one of the men pointed a stubby handgun at them.

The woman felt the blood drain from her face.

113

'Stay quiet and no one will get hurt,' said the gunman. Rain dripped off his yellow coat onto the pale carpet.

The other burglar pushed past them and went over to pick up the box on the sofa.

'Hand over your valuables and no one gets hurt,' said the gunman. He nudged the woman with the stubby end of the weapon and she whimpered.

Reluctantly her husband stood back, letting them take the box. The burglar turned it upside down. The slim black jewellery boxes fell out on top of the passports and certificates. He picked up the jewellery and stashed it in his jacket pockets. He left the rest, and gestured to his partner.

'That's it. All done here.'

'See?' said the gunman. 'Painless if you let us get on with it.'

And the intruders climbed back out of the window and joined their partner in the boat.

As they started up the engine, they could hear the woman sobbing.

'Better get away from here,' said the gunman. 'She's screaming the place down and the neighbours might hear.'

The other man took the jewel cases out of his pockets and put them in a rucksack on the floor of the boat.

The burglars had been at a boat show in Earl's Court when the flood struck. As well as the small motorboat they'd got the yellow coats, some binoculars – and the flare pistol, which was proving extremely useful. Since then, they had visited so many people that afternoon, all of them rescuing their valuables from their safes; all of them sitting ducks for burglars.

The gunman was now focusing the binoculars down the street. 'I think our next stop should be that big house at the end of the road,' he said. 'I can see a lady waiting for us with a leather briefcase . . .'

Chapter Fifteen

Bel was not at Charing Cross, waiting for Ben.

She wanted to be, but she was still stuck in Westminster – though at the present moment she wasn't quite sure *where* in Westminster.

The room was small – about five metres square. It contained a desk, a telephone and several chairs. It reminded Bel of a dentist's waiting room, except she had never been in a waiting room that had blank concrete walls and no windows. The only thing to look at was the two sets of doors.

One set led to a stairwell. That's where they had come in. The other doors were massive and thick, with steel bars and rivets. They reminded Bel of the blast doors she had seen in the Tube.

One minute she had been in a meeting room in the Cabinet Office, waiting for the Prime Minister of Canada to arrive and talking to Clive Brooks and Sidney Cadogan, his boss from the Department of the Environment.

The next minute some alarms had gone off and a plainclothes policeman had come in and asked them to follow him.

He had ushered them into a corridor full of security men – plainclothes policemen with handguns bulging under their jackets. They were searching the offices and evacuating any members of staff they found.

Bel and the others were escorted to a door with a sign on it saying 'NO ADMITTANCE'. The Foreign Secretary, Madeleine Harwood, was already waiting there. She was a plump woman in a tweed suit, but not the trendy kind; it was the kind worn by fierce headmistresses. The 'NO ADMITTANCE' door was unlocked and they were told to go through.

Bel thought it must be a bomb scare. She followed a policeman and Sidney Cadogan down a narrow flight of concrete stairs that went down and down and down. Madeleine Harwood puffed behind, complaining that she was getting dizzy.

The policeman was waiting for them beside another open door, this time leading to another set of stairs. The journey down continued. Finally they had ended up in this room.

Sidney Cadogan looked the most at home. He sat in one of the plastic chairs, one suited leg crossed over the other to reveal socks in fine grey wool and a black polished shoe. The sole was biscuit-coloured leather and embossed with the name Church's. It looked so clean that Bel thought he must levitate everywhere, or at least only walk on carpets.

Madeleine Harwood sat beside Sidney, trying to appear as cool, but not quite managing. She kept smoothing down the skirt of her tweed suit and looking nervously at the big door. Clive Brooks sat opposite, running his hand through his thinning badger hair.

Bel didn't know how any of them could sit still. She wanted to pace but there wasn't any room. She rolled the sleeves of her purple suit up to her elbows, her classic gesture of impatience, and stood near the blast door with the policeman, studying it.

'So where are we?' she asked. 'Buckingham Palace's secret bunker?'

Sidney Cadogan answered. 'Ten floors beneath the Cabinet Office.'

'What's happened?' Madeleine Harwood asked the policeman. 'Is it a bomb threat? A fire drill?'

'I think it's a flood.'

That surprised them all. Bel frowned. 'A flood? How bad?'

'I believe Downing Street is under water. But they'll probably have more details when we get inside.'

'Inside where?' said Bel.

A green light came on over the blast doors. Slowly they opened. Beyond was a corridor with a row of lights along the ceiling.

'Follow me, please,' said the policeman.

They followed him into a cylindrical tunnel. It was lined with rings of concrete bolted together.

'Are we in the Tube?' said Bel.

'No,' said Sidney Cadogan. His tone said, *Don't ask any more questions.*

'Well, where are we?' said Bel, irritated. 'It's a bit late to be secretive now, Sidney. I'm already here.'

They came to three signs. One pointed right, to Horse Guards Parade. The middle one pointed straight ahead to 10 Downing Street, which was blocked off with another set of blast doors.

Madeleine Harwood looked at the signs with sudden recognition. 'This is Q-Whitehall.'

'That's right,' said Clive Brooks. 'Haven't you been down here yet?'

'You know I only took up office last month,' she told him. 'No one's had time to give me the tour yet.'

Sidney glared at her as though she had betrayed some great secret. 'Be careful what you say, Madeleine,' he said.

Bel thought he was being an idiot. 'Sidney, I hate to disillusion you, but kids talk about Q-Whitehall on the Internet. It's no big secret. You ought to get out more.'

The policeman took them down the left-hand branch, signed 'Ministry of Defence'.

'If they're discussing Q-Whitehall,' said Sidney, 'that's because we allow them to.'

Bel would never normally have let such a pompous

remark go unpunished, but she was wrestling with some far more unpleasant thoughts. It had suddenly struck her. When the policeman had said Downing Street was flooded, she'd assumed it was just that small area – a water main burst or something. Now she realized that was dumb. They wouldn't have come down into this complex if it had just been a minor utilities problem. This had to be a major flood.

She tapped the policeman on the shoulder. 'How widespread is the flooding?'

'It's pretty bad, ma'am.'

'Is it on the south bank as well?'

'I don't know, ma'am.' They came to another set of blast doors. The policeman opened a flap in the wall and keyed in a pass code. He waited for a green light, then keyed in another combination. The doors began to vibrate and swung slowly open. They heard voices. Quite a lot of voices.

Like the worries chattering in Bel's mind. She'd been talking about London flooding on *News Focus* the other day. Without the Thames Barrier a lot of central London would be underwater, she'd said. They were her own words, coming back to haunt her.

She wondered about Ben. Was he safe? The ArBonCo Centre was a tall building. If Ben just stayed there with Cally, he would be all right – Cally would have looked after him; she wouldn't let anything happen to him, she thought.

'Impressive, isn't it?' said Clive Brooks. He obviously mistook Bel's silence for amazement.

'All the people from the MoD building must already be down here,' said Sidney. 'I hope they haven't got the best bunks.'

They were directed to a table like a reception desk, and a man in a security armband looked up at them.

'Another party from the Cabinet Office,' said the policeman.

The man behind the desk passed a clipboard to Sidney. 'We need you all to sign in so we can keep track of who's down here. Once you've checked in, please keep together.'

Sidney handed the clipboard to Madeleine. 'Ladies first.'

Madeleine looked at Sidney frostily. 'Don't patronize me, Sidney,' she told him, but she took the clipboard, then passed it to Bel.

She signed in, then waited for the others. Next to her she saw a room marked as the library. It was a small block of a room with a low ceiling, as if someone had buried a concrete shoebox. The lighting was cold and clinical. It made her think of being in an underground car park.

She spotted a map on the wall and went over to study it. The structure seemed to be a series of boxes connected by tunnels. There was a dining hall, common room one, common room two, two cinemas. Loads of storerooms, two generator rooms, air-conditioning plant, fuel store. One section was sleeping accommodation: small, cramped cabins like a row of lockers. The place looked like it was equipped to outlast a nuclear winter.

There was another map too, which showed how that section fitted into a much bigger tunnel system. There was the entrance they had used, by the crossroads leading to Horse Guards Parade and Downing Street. Further away there were more exits all over central London. One came out at Charing Cross.

Bel grabbed one of the plainclothes policemen. 'Can I get out that way?' she asked him, pointing at the map.

'There's no way out now, ma'am. All the exits are sealed until the all-clear.'

Bel saw Sidney Cadogan pulling Madeleine Harwood to one side. 'Madeleine, you'd better come this way,' he said to her. 'It looks like you're the most senior minister here.'

She quickly started to follow as he ushered Madeleine and Clive through a door marked 'BRIEFING ROOM'.

'Sidney, does that mean you're in contact with the outside world?' she asked him.

Sidney gave her his most saccharine smile. 'Authorized personnel only, I'm afraid. Unless we call you in.' And he pulled the door shut.

Bel stuck her foot in the way. 'I need to know how bad the flooding is on the south bank. My son is in the ArBonCo Centre. Is there a phone anywhere?'

The plainclothes policeman gently pulled her back. 'There are no phones, ma'am. We'll give you any news as soon as we get it.'

Chapter Sixteen

The beat of helicopters taking off drowned out everything in the controller's headphones for a moment. He was in the emergency special operations room in the basement of the police training college in Hendon, north London, well away from the flood. The emergency – a Code Red – was too big for the normal emergency services to handle and the armed forces had been drafted in to support them.

The controller, who was co-ordinating the emergency response, was a senior police officer. Right now he was on satellite link to Royal Naval Air Station Yeovilton in Somerset.

The noise of the helicopter faded. 'Sorry, Yeovilton, can you repeat?'

'Thirty Sea Kings are on their way to you. We're keeping five to cover the coast – the sea defences are looking ropey down here.'

'Thank you, Yeovilton.' The controller switched to the next channel. 'Hampshire, this is Hendon. What have you got for us?'

'Thirty Chinooks on their way to you, Hendon.'

He switched again, to Royal Navy Force Deployment in Northwood, just up the road in Middlesex.

'Twenty Sea Kings on their way to you now, sir.'

'Roger.'

He cut the connection and sat back, slipping his headphones off. Behind him, two men in formal, high-ranking uniforms had been observing: the Chief Commissioner of the Metropolitan Police, and General Thomas Chambers, the Head of the Armed Forces.

The controller's assistant also took off his headset and spoke to the Chief and the General. 'Sir, we've got twenty-five more Pumas and Merlins from Northern Ireland – they'll be with us in four hours' time.'

'Very good,' said General Chambers.

'The flood area is now clear of all non-essential air traffic,' said another assistant. 'All commercial flights passing over London are being diverted.'

'Sir,' called a female engineer in an army uniform. 'We've got the satellite pictures.'

The Chief Commissioner and General Chambers went across and looked over her shoulder. The devastation was even worse than they had feared.

From Brixton to Westminster, from Greenwich to Shepherd's Bush, London was underwater.

Another soldier came up and spoke to them. 'Satellite link to Q-Whitehall is up and running, sir.'

'About time,' said General Chambers. 'Has the Prime Minister been informed yet?'

'Not yet, sir. We're trying to get onto him. He had a confidential meeting this morning at Chequers.'

General Chambers and the Chief Commissioner followed the soldier to a workstation. On the screen, they could see a room in the bunker – and a row of faces sitting at the table facing the camera. General Chambers spoke into the microphone. 'I need a minister with authority over Rebro. Where's the Home Secretary?'

On the screen Madeleine Harwood spoke up. 'I'm the Foreign Secretary. I'm the only minister in the offices today. Is everything under control?'

The Chief Commissioner took the microphone. 'We're going to switch off Rebro and we need you to authorize it.'

Madeleine Harwood looked baffled. 'Rebro?'

Clive Brooks explained. 'The emergency services' communications network. It's been running on back-up. We've got rescue helicopters coming in and we need the power supply for our satellite communications so that we can co-ordinate the rescue operation. We can't run Rebro as well. You have to give us permission to switch it off.'

General Chambers took the microphone. 'It's not a big problem, ma'am. The ambulances, fire engines and police cars won't be able to communicate with each other. But half the roads are underwater and the ones that aren't are gridlocked. They can't do their job anyway so we're sending the army in. That's why I'm here with the Chief Commissioner.'

Madeleine Harwood folded her arms. 'Why do you need me to give the order? You're the experts.'

'Because in theory there are consequences for the civilian population and that's not a decision we can make. The decision has to be made by the government. Are you giving the order?'

Madeleine clearly wasn't happy but she knew she had no choice but to act decisively and trust the experts. 'All right. I'm authorizing you to switch it off.'

'Thank you, madam.' The General cut the audio connection to the bunker and spoke to the rest of the room. 'Close down Rebro. Divert power to satellite communications.'

Fingers flew over keyboards, orders were spoken into headsets as the emergency room staff made the necessary adjustments.

The Chief Commissioner looked thoughtful. 'General Chambers, once we've rescued the immediate casualties we're going to need to think about evacuating the civilian population.'

The General considered this for a moment, then turned to speak to a woman manning a workstation behind him. 'Lieutenant,' he ordered, bending down to speak to her. 'I want you to concentrate on getting hold of the Prime Minister.'

'Very good, sir.'

Chapter Seventeen

Ben was warmer now, and at least the Burberry stopped him getting any wetter. To his right he saw the water covering the road like a black slick; beyond the buildings the swollen river spread out like a loch.

Above him he could hear a new sound through the beat of the rain. A thrumming, like a helicopter but at the same time not quite like one.

A dark shape was moving across above the river. Red lights winked on its underside and Ben saw short helicopter rotors whirling round at each end. A Chinook. The rescue effort must be starting.

It paused over the water, framed for a moment by

the gap between the buildings, then began to descend. Ben dashed across the road and waved, but the Chinook was aiming for the roof of a low building surrounded by water, where a group of people were stranded like penguins on an iceberg. It stopped and hovered about ten metres above the roof, its side door open. Ben could see people moving inside; then a winchman on a harness dropped out of the doorway and swung down to the figures on the roof.

He heard another double-beat of helicopter blades. A second Chinook went over, heading west, upriver. It was like being in a war movie, Ben thought.

And he was still on his own.

He stopped to turn the page of the *A–Z*. The pages were wet, stuck together like tissue paper. He peeled them apart carefully, worried about tearing them. The printing from the other side of the page was showing through anyway, making it hopelessly confusing. On the opposite side of the road was a high wall with metal spikes along the top. If he remembered correctly that was the grounds of Buckingham Palace. He put the *A–Z* back in his pocket, decided to keep the wall to his right and started walking again.

Standing still even for that short time had made him shivery, so he hurried along, trying to warm up again. Suddenly, as he looked more closely along a side street, he saw rats scuttling along, away from the water. He shivered. He also noticed manhole covers littering the street and Ben wondered why. They must have been lifted by the pressure of the water as it rose up out of the drains. That made him wish his dad was with him because they would have chatted about it.

Ben's thoughts returned to Bel. If she could have been a normal mother and stayed at home, Ben wouldn't be here right now. But she wanted to be mother to the entire planet's ecosystem, nagging everyone to take better care of it and telling them they'd regret it if they didn't. Now Ben was trudging through these wet streets with no money and no way of getting in touch with anybody. It was as if her long years of doom-mongering had conjured up the whole disaster. She'd said everyone would suffer and now they were doing just that. He hoped she was out there in the rain too, getting the full benefit. She certainly deserved to be.

* * *

The winch operator on the Chinook slowly wound the sling back up. In the harness on the end, the winchman was a soldier, his head encased in a green helmet like a cannonball with his surname painted on the back. He was carrying an exhausted woman, his arms and legs supporting her so that she didn't slip. The sling swung in the air currents set up by the rotors, and khaki-sleeved arms reached down to pull it in.

As soon as the woman was safely clear of the door, two medics knelt down to examine her. Above the whine of the engines they couldn't speak, but they didn't need to. Her blue lips and delayed response to her surroundings were classic signs of hypothermia. One medic spread a khaki blanket over her while another took her pulse.

While they worked on her, a row of people who had been rescued watched as they sat huddled in foil survival blankets against the bare metal ribs of the fuselage. The craft was huge and was carrying about fifty casualties; some of them on canvas stretchers, others clutching warm drinks. Another medic kept an eye on them, taking their pulses, tending to injuries.

The inside of the Chinook smelled of dirty water

and worse: sewage. London's sewers had disgorged their contents into the streets. It wasn't good news: stopping infection and disease was going to be a big problem over the days to come.

At the door, the winch operator and the winchman were checking their equipment, ready to make another journey, but then the co-pilot tapped the winchman on the shoulder and gave a throat-cutting gesture with his hand. No more rescues. They were full. He gave another hand signal: close the doors. The winch operator nodded and went to secure the sling. As his partner closed the doors, he could see more people down below, waving out of windows, standing on roofs. There was a couple stuck on the roof of their car, the vehicle a tiny red island in a lake of filthy water. As the Chinook gained height, the figures who still needed help dwindled to specks.

As they left the flooded area, London began to look more normal again. But they saw that every street was packed with cars, a daisy chain of brake lights as people tried to escape the city. Some of them had their possessions tied to their roofs, like giant snails. They might as well have been snails for all the progress they were making. The wet air was grey with smog from their chugging engines.

The winchman was looking out of the other window with binoculars. He turned to hand them to his partner and pointed out of the window.

Beside the stationary line of traffic was a grey-brown, moving mass. At first it looked like running water, but it seemed to be grainy, as though it was composed of many small pieces.

He focused the binoculars and realized what it was. *Rats*. They must have come out of the sewers. They were swarming past the stationary cars.

That seemed to sum up the day. When the rats decided to leave London, there really was no going back.

Chapter Eighteen

The undercarriage of the Flying Eye touched down at last in Stapleford Aerodrome in Essex. As Mike slowed the plane to taxi speed, he and Meena both felt they'd come to the end of a long journey. They were lucky the airfield was still there; quite a lot of the surrounding countryside was underwater and the nearby river Lee had burst its banks. But everything at the airfield looked normal: the control tower, the hangars, the sprinkling of cars in the car park.

Meena unbuckled her seatbelt and looked through her pictures.

'Did they come out?' said Mike. 'You owe me a drink for those.'

Meena grinned at him. 'When I collect my Press Association award, you can be my guest at the ceremony.' She heard a crackle coming from her headphones on the dashboard. 'Hey, Capital's transmitting again.' She lifted the cups to her ears, then frowned and routed the radio through the plane's speakers. 'Listen to this.'

It was a strange serious-sounding voice, like a BBC news reader's. '. . . *important to turn off gas and electricity, if it is safe to do so. If you are stranded in a building and your exit is flooded, you can alert the rescue parties by hanging a sheet or large piece of cloth out of the window. Do not go out unless it is absolutely necessary.*'

'That's not Capital,' said Mike.

Meena checked the tuning. 'It's on the Capital frequency.'

'*Do not try to wade through the water or swim as the current is dangerous. Even twenty centimetres of water can knock you off your feet. Do not try to improvize boats with paddling pools or other items, or use recreational swimming toys such as lilos or air beds. You are much safer staying where you are and waiting for the rescue services to come to you.'*

'Where did they get him?' said Mike. 'He sounds like he came out of a time warp.'

Meena tried twiddling the dial. 'LBC's out. Oh – Radio One's on. But it's playing the same thing.'

'The emergency services must have taken over the transmitters.'

'How do they do that, then? The Capital offices were abandoned.'

'They've probably got a way to cover a range of frequencies. Or something. I don't know. I'm only a pilot.'

'If you are in a building whose lower floors are flooded, try to dress warmly: if your building is flooded, the water will cool it down. Try to find loose-fitting, comfortable garments and good walking shoes. If you need medicines, make sure they are close at hand. You can make sandbags to stop water coming in under doors, using pillows or cushions or heavy material such as blankets.'

Mike brought the plane to a halt, went through

the power-down procedure and opened the door.

Meena remained sitting in the seat, her eyes fixed on the pictures on her camera.

'What's up? Did you leave the lens cap on?'

'I'll be OK in a minute.'

For the first time Meena began to realize what she had just seen. London was wrecked. She'd grown up there, built a career there. She didn't live there now, but so many people she knew did. Many of her favourite places were there: shops, theatres, cafés, restaurants, museums. The landmarks of London were the landmarks of her life. With a heavy heart she climbed down from the plane.

'Miss?'

A man in army fatigues was walking out of the hangar. He had a green helmet under his arm with the name DOREK handpainted on it in white letters, and seemed to be looking straight at her.

'Yes?'

'Are those pictures of the disaster area?' His accent was Polish.

'Yes, they are.'

'The emergency services would be very interested in

them. We need to make a map of the disaster area and any information at all is being considered of value at present.'

She sighed and held her camera up. 'You're welcome to them, if you can find a printer.'

There was not a helicopter in sight at the Royal Naval Air Station at Yeovilton. The rain fell on a mass of empty tarmac. Junior communications officer Lieutenant William Beaumont had never seen it empty like that. Every single heli was out on a mission. And that meant the communications room was stretched to the limit.

'I'm sorry, sir,' said Beaumont to his captain, 'we don't have enough bandwidth to send that message at present.'

The captain needed to get his message to General Chambers in Hendon. 'Just find a way to send it, Lieutenant, it's top priority.'

'With respect, sir,' said Beaumont, 'all the satellites are fully in use.' He indicated his workstation, where he was tracking all the helicopters that had been dispatched to deal with the emergency.

The captain clearly didn't believe him. He sighed, then bent down and hit a couple of keys on Beaumont's workstation. The display changed. The lieutenant was annoyed but there was nothing he could do about it: the captain was his superior.

The captain's finger stabbed the screen. 'There. That channel's free. Send it on that.'

'You can't use that channel, sir,' said Beaumont. 'It has to be kept clear for vital defence communications.'

'This *is* a vital communication, Lieutenant. Now just send it. That's an order.'

In the cold rolling waters of the Atlantic Ocean, a black shape emerged. It looked like a shark's fin, but much bigger. A radio antenna rose slowly out of the top, in a tube camouflaged with white and black so that it blended into the sea and sky around it.

The object was speeding through the water, the waves closing over it as it went. When the waves rolled away, a little more became visible – the top of something much bigger, long and dark: a hundred and fifty metres long – longer than a football pitch. It was HMS *Vanquish*, a Vanguard-class nuclear submarine.

The captain stood on the bridge, or conn, hands on hips, bathed in red light. It was dark and cramped there and it smelled of oil and sweat. The walls of instruments twinkled with coloured lights and glowing screens. It was also noisy with radio static, the steady bleep of the sonar and the thrum of the propeller that drove the craft through the water.

The helmsman was watching a readout of the sub's depth. 'We're on the surface now, sir.'

'Antenna is deployed and active,' said the communications officer.

The submarine had several systems of communication. There was the VLF antenna by the conning tower. VLF stood for Very Low Frequency, the only type of radio signals that could penetrate water. This was how the sub kept in contact with its commanders in the UK. Because the frequency was so low, it could not carry audio signals like voices, so most orders and routine transmissions from the UK were sent as encrypted text. Then there was a buoyant wire antenna – an aerial several hundred metres long that floated up on a cable like a tail and allowed the sub to pick up transmissions without surfacing. And, for use in special circumstances, there was an erectable mast in the top fin. To use this mast, the sub had to be able to surface.

At the moment the *Vanquish* was testing all three systems. Every four hours it received a standard message from its commanders in the Admiralty; an all-clear to let them know that all was well in the UK. The transmission was top priority and was never missed.

But the last one had failed to come through.

'Commence testing,' said the captain.

'Testing now, sir.'

The communications officer sent a test signal and monitored the three receivers for the results. They were all fine. He turned round. 'Sir, all communications equipment is fully operational. There is no reason why we should have missed the transmission.'

'Thank you, Officer.' The captain unhooked a microphone attached to his command post by a curly cable and spoke into it. 'Computer room, this is the captain. Are there any malfunctions on the communications equipment?'

'No malfunctions, sir. All systems are working correctly.'

The captain slipped the microphone back to his command station. He was aware that the eyes of all the crew members were on him.

'Communications Officer, is there anything else we can do to re-establish communication?'

'No, sir. But sir – I'm picking up radio broadcasts saying London is submerged. There may have been some kind of natural disaster there.'

The captain thought. 'Gentlemen, we have our protocols and we must follow them. We have strict instructions on what to do if our all-clear transmission is missed. That is so that if there is an emergency, High Command know exactly what we will do. We will have to risk exposing our position by sending a signal to High Command. Communications Officer, send the emergency message.'

The communications officer was ready. He rapidly typed the message into his keyboard and watched the thermometer bar on the screen as it was fired off into the ether. 'Message successfully sent, sir.'

The message sent, they could submerge once more. 'Dive to three hundred metres. Full speed ahead.'

'Aye-aye, Captain.'

They all felt the pressure in their ears as the ship began to submerge. There was another feeling too: a deep shudder as the propeller bit into the sea. With a Chinagraph pencil the navigator made notes about their course on a Perspex map.

The captain unhooked the intercom again and spoke to the ship. 'This is the captain. Our routine all-clear transmission from High Command has been missed and we have had to break cover by contacting them. This has exposed our presence in these waters. We are now in a vulnerable position as we could be targeted by enemy action. We do not know the reason why High Command has missed the routine all-clear transmission. Until we contact them, this boat is in a state of emergency. Everyone will work double shifts and all privileges are cancelled.'

Lieutenant Roberts was coming off duty in the computer room and intending to grab a bite to eat in the mess. Now he hurried down faster than usual. Privileges cancelled meant no watching movies or time off. What on earth was going on?

The cramped mess was crowded when he got there.

Midshipmen, oilers and officers were all trying to grab a quick bite before going straight back on duty.

Roberts grabbed some rather grey-looking stew and a couple of rolls and sat down opposite Andrews, a missiles engineer, who was trying to shovel soup and a sandwich into his mouth as fast as humanly possible. They were also discussing the captain's announcement.

'What do you think's happened in England?' said Roberts. 'Why didn't we get our all-clear?'

Andrews stuffed the last of his corned-beef sandwich into his mouth and stole some of Roberts's bread roll. 'I bet some idiot in the Admiralty has used the secure frequency to phone their girlfriend, or some other SNAFU. But this *could* be serious. We don't know what's happened up there. The next eight hours or so will be critical. If we can't contact Whitehall we could even end up launching missiles. After all, that's what we're here for. We're carrying four nukes.'

Nukes; nuclear warheads. HMS *Vanquish* had the capacity to carry sixteen Trident II D-5 missiles, which could each carry twelve warheads . . .

Chapter Nineteen

In Hendon, General Thomas Chambers had been on the satellite link with Chequers. He had some information about the Prime Minister, but it wasn't helpful. He wasn't in a top-secret meeting. He had taken off from Chequers that morning in a helicopter. Now General Chambers was waiting for staff at Chequers to get back to him with the flight plan.

Right now, they were having another conversation he'd hoped to avoid. The chief commissioner was trying to persuade the politicians and civil servants in the bunker at Whitehall to give the go-ahead to evacuate the city.

The Foreign Secretary and the two grey-haired civil servants had been joined by a fat man in a pinstripe suit, who General Chambers recognized as a back-bench MP.

'If we evacuate London,' said Fat Pinstripe, 'it could wipe billions off the stock market. It's just unnecessary.'

The general could see someone behind him. She was only visible from chest to mid-thigh, as she paced in and out of shot, continually rolling up the sleeves of a crumpled purple suit. 'The world will have seen the news pictures by now,' she said testily. 'You're not going to stop people finding out.' Her tone was haranguing; it sounded vaguely familiar.

Fat Pinstripe didn't seem to be taking much notice of her. He turned to Sidney Cadogan and Clive Brooks. 'It's a disgrace that they don't keep us better informed down here. When we get out, we'd better make sure they improve things. We can't be left out of the loop like this. We haven't had any proper debate. A decision to evacuate needs proper debate.'

'You've been institutionalized too long,' said Purple Sleeves. 'This is real life, not your cosy House of Commons debating club.'

Fat Pinstripe turned round and addressed her directly. 'It's you who seems to be playing to the audience, Doctor Kelland. You're not on *News Focus* now. This issue hasn't been thought through. If we evacuate, where are we going to put them all?'

She came back at him immediately. 'Where are we going to put all the bodies if they're dead?' She sat down, shaking her head angrily. 'You asked me to join you for my knowledge of this kind of scenario – just what we've been predicting could happen for years. But now you're not even listening. You've *got* to evacuate. I've seen situations like this before – and computer models of even more. The sewers will be flooding and disease will start to spread. It's summer. Yes, it's not a nice summer, but it's still warm. Bacteria are going to be breeding like wildfire in that water. And what about drinking water?'

Madeleine Harwood cut in at this point. 'Can't you just follow emergency procedures?' she asked.

The chief commissioner kept his voice even. 'Yes, once you give the order to evacuate.'

There was a silence. Madeleine Harwood caught the eye of the other woman, who didn't say anything but her face dared the Minister to back out. 'Evacuate London,' said the Foreign Secretary after a long pause.

The chief commissioner cut the connection and addressed the room at Hendon. 'The government has given the go-ahead to evacuate London.'

The controller took his headphones off. 'Sir, we're barely coping with the rescues. We just haven't got the manpower to evacuate seven and a half million people.'

'*Do not drive unless your journey is absolutely necessary. If you come across a flooded area, take care.*'

Ben heard the voice and peered into the shop. It was a sculptor's studio. A figure made of plaster and wire stood in the window, against a backdrop of oyster-coloured silk.

The door was open, the studio dark except for a soft blue light coming from the radio playing on a shelf.

'*Do not drive through any water if you don't know how deep it is. Do not attempt to drive through fast-moving water. Keep in a low gear and drive slowly and evenly to avoid creating a bow wave . . .'*

That blue display light was such a welcoming sight and the voice on the radio was authoritative and reassuring. Ben cautiously went through the door. 'Hello? Is there anyone there?' he called.

The studio was dominated by a table that ran the length of the room. Scattered on it were hammers, chisels, lengths of wire wrapped around card. In the centre was a shape vaguely like a horse's head, made of wire.

'Allow oncoming traffic to pass first . . .'

He didn't hear the movement behind him. Suddenly his arm was grabbed and twisted painfully backwards. He felt something hard digging into his back and a voice hissed in his ear. It had an accent – European-sounding; perhaps Spanish. It smelled of strong cigarettes.

'Keep quiet and do as I say.'

On the radio the quiet voice continued. '*Keep revving and slipping the clutch, otherwise water could enter the exhaust. If your car stalls, abandon it and climb to higher ground.*'

Ben felt like his arm would be dislocated at any

moment. He spluttered out a reply. 'I'm sorry, I just wanted to get out of the rain. I haven't touched anything. I'll go.'

'Stay still.'

Ben nodded And the pressure on his arms eased, although his captor kept hold of one wrist. Ben moved cautiously, stretching out his shoulders. That had really hurt. The last thing he wanted to do was provoke another attack and be subjected to that pain again.

'*Once you are through the water,*' said the calm voice on the radio, '*test your brakes as soon as you can.*'

'Turn round,' said the Spanish voice. The man kept hold of Ben's wrist.

As Ben did so, he caught sight of the studio door again. There was a ragged hole where the lock had been. The Spanish man wasn't the sculptor defending his art; he had broken in.

Ben's captor was in silhouette, his back to the open door. He must have done that so that he could see Ben, while Ben couldn't see very much of him. He smelled of river water and drains and his clothes were stuck to him. Like Ben, he had been caught in the flood.

'We're walking.' He jerked Ben's wrist, then dragged him along past the long table towards the back of the studio. Ben banged his shins against something on the floor. They came to a door and the man kicked it open, let go of Ben's wrist and pushed him through.

Ahead was a dingy corridor; on a shelf sat a grubby kettle and a chipped mug, plus a box of tea bags. A staircase led to an upper floor, while under the stairs Ben saw another door.

The Spaniard turned Ben around and he saw that the man's wrists were handcuffed and bloody. He was holding something, a sharp serrated object: a hacksaw.

He held out his hands towards Ben, stretching them apart so that the chain link between the cuffs was taut. 'Cut them apart,' he ordered.

Ben had no thoughts of disobeying. He couldn't run off now – the man was blocking his exit. And anyway, he looked strong and tough, even if he was handcuffed. He took the hacksaw, positioned it and started working it to and fro. The man stood looking at his hands impassively. Ben didn't think about what he was doing, or why the man was handcuffed: he just wanted to get it over with as fast as possible.

The man had obviously already tried to get the cuffs off by other means; his wrists were raw and red and there was a gash across the back of his hand where he had tried to get something under a cuff to force it open. Ben felt his eyes glowering at him as he worked. Deep-set eyes, dark brows and black hair. And he was clearly used to making other people do what he wanted. Judging by the blood on his wrists he could put up with a fair degree of discomfort too.

Ben sawed on. The handle of the saw was biting into his hands, but he didn't dare stop. The blade became hot, but finally it had cut through the link.

The Spaniard pulled his wrists apart savagely, grabbed the hacksaw from Ben and threw it out into the dark shop. Ben was suddenly terrified by the new look of purpose in his eyes. What was he going to do now?

The man grabbed Ben's arm and twisted it up again. As before, the pain in Ben's shoulder told him to go with it or risk breaking something.

This time he found himself forced down to his knees. But that seemed to be what the man wanted because the pressure eased immediately.

Then he pulled open the door under the stairs and twisted Ben's arm again. Again the pain. Ben guessed he was meant to go through the door. He was reduced to the level of an automaton, his arm like a lever – press for go, press for stop. He stumbled forwards and grabbed for the wall as he saw a flight of steps going down in front of him. He must be in a cellar.

Then the door was slammed and a key turned. Ben was locked in. And it was pitch-black.

He put his ear to the door and heard things tumbling from shelves as the man moved back through the studio. Either he was very clumsy or he was helping himself to the tools on the workbench. After a moment he heard the front door slam shut.

Then there was silence, except for the sound of the radio, softly playing its reassuring messages.

'*There is no need for panic. The police are still in control. Law and order has not broken down.*'

Like hell, thought Ben. His body started to shiver violently, like it was in the grip of a fit. He realized how frightened he had been. He'd literally come out in a cold sweat.

Suddenly he heard something that made him go even colder. Somewhere down the cellar steps in the darkness there was a splash.

There was water down there.

And something moving.

Chapter Twenty

Outside, Francisco Gomez shrugged his shoulders, easing the movement back into his arms. A rucksack hung from his hand, filled with screwdrivers, a Stanley knife and other useful items from the sculptor's studio. He'd also found a warm navy blue jacket so at least he could keep warm. Best of all, he'd picked up a tattered A–Z that was lying on the floor. It was soggy with rain.

When he floated away from the police station on the park bench, he'd drifted through the streets of Chelsea for quite a way. He was at the mercy of the water because of his handcuffs, so had to pick his moment to jump off. Eventually the bench got caught against some iron railings outside one of the grand town houses. He didn't know where he was so he waded for quite some way to make sure he was well out of the district and to get clear of the flood water before trying to get rid of the handcuffs. Now he was a free man. Thank goodness for the British weather.

That *A–Z* was a useful find. He looked at it, got the information he needed, then tossed it in a bin. It had even been open on the page he needed: Charing Cross Station. That was where he was heading for. There were things he had to collect there. Things he had put away in case he had to flee Britain suddenly. And things his partner would need too – if he was free as well by now. They were professionals; they always had a plan and a course of action to follow whatever happened, and he knew José would stick to it just as he was. If everything went as he hoped, they would rendezvous shortly and then make their escape . . .

'The Paddington branch of the Grand Union Canal has flooded and there are barges stranded on the railway line.'

Meena Chohan never thought she'd be back in the air so quickly. When the soldiers printed out her pictures, they had shown useful detail not available in the satellite pictures – but there weren't enough of them. So here she was up in the cockpit of a Puma helicopter, talking through a headset to an army cartographer in the seat behind, who was working on a battery-operated laptop. Using her detailed knowledge of London, they were creating a map of the disaster zone, marking areas with flooding so that they could co-ordinate evacuation services. They also needed to mark significant vehicle wreckage and traffic congestion which would result in rescue vehicles not being able to gain access.

It was like doing the usual daily traffic report, but bizarrely different. The transformation of the city was stunning. The river was at least ten times as wide as normal, its distinctive kinks completely gone. She had mixed feelings about it. One part of her was impatient to get her pictures to a newsroom before someone else pipped her to the post. Another part was already imagining how she would write up this trip as a much better, much bigger story.

The water was full of debris. Once again she was astounded by the sight of the wreckage. Cars, buses and lorries turned on their sides, on their backs, piled up against the walls of buildings.

The cartographer, whose name was Phil, was keying in the information. There was a grinding sound as he saved the file to disk, then he tapped the pilot on the shoulder and gave him the thumbs-up. 'Nearly done. I've just got to process it now. Fly around in a circle for a bit while I see if there are any gaps.'

The pilot had his name – Dorek – handpainted on the back of his helmet; he twitched the control stick between his knees and swung round in a loop. Down below, Meena could see rows of army vehicles and big canvas tents pitched on Hampstead Heath. It looked like a giant khaki circus. The incessant rain pooled in the roofs of the tents like lakes, reflecting the Puma as it passed overhead.

Another helicopter, a Sea King, had obviously just landed there. Soldiers were helping civilians out, hurrying them towards the tents. Everyone looked soaking wet.

'What's going on there?' said Meena.

'That's where they're taking evacuees from the flooded area,' said Dorek.

They circled back to the flood zone, flying over a series of low flat-roofed buildings at the water's edge. On one roof a soldier was dragging along something that looked like a man, leaving heel marks in the gravel surface. As Meena watched, he propped him up at the edge of the roof and buttoned his jacket round the railings to keep him there. Another soldier was tying a red marker to the TV aerial.

'I'll mark that one,' said Phil.

A cold feeling crept all the way up Meena's back. 'What are they doing?' she asked.

'We can't move all the bodies yet,' said Dorek. 'So we're putting them in easily accessible places to pick up later.'

'Why are they being tied to the railings?'

'In case there's another surge. Now we've got them in one place we don't want them floating away some- where by themselves. It's just to keep them out of everyone's way really.'

Meena looked out of the other window and spotted

what she thought were more bodies below. 'Oh, there's another lot,' she said.

Phil followed her gaze. 'No, no. It's the Chelsea Pensioners. See if they need a hand.'

Dorek took them in lower, over a big, sprawling building. It was the Royal Hospital, Chelsea, home of the Chelsea Pensioners. Some figures in red coats were using a window-cleaner's cradle to hoist some bedraggled figures in civvies up to the top floor.

'It looks as though they've got things under control,' said the pilot. 'They're rescuing a load of civilians.'

The Chelsea Pensioners? thought Meena. She had a mental picture of frail old men in red coats with shiny buttons and war ribbons and black tricorn hats, shaking hands with the Queen at the Chelsea Flower Show. 'I thought those guys were about seventy,' she said.

'They're tough old guys,' chuckled Dorek. 'Hold tight.' He slid the Puma down sideways. The down-draught made ripple patterns in the rain-spattered water. He nudged the control stick and the Puma tilted from side to side and then flew level again.

The pensioners recognized the salute and gave a thumbs-up in return.

'They seem to be doing fine,' said Dorek, and headed downriver again. They flew on, passing over the bulk of St Thomas's Hospital, water lapping all around the building, and he banked for the return journey.

'I'm just sending the map now,' said Phil. 'We're done here.' He tapped some keys and sent the map by secure satellite e-mail.

Dorek pulled away and sped up, back towards Essex.

Down below in the hospital, the medical staff were doing their best in the difficult circumstances. A nurse wearing theatre scrubs, a torch strapped to her fore-head, was bending over a patient, squeezing a plastic bottle in a slow, regular rhythm. A tube led from the bottle into the patient's throat. He had been on the operating table when the power cuts came, plunging them into darkness.

It was freezing cold in the recovery room. The water that had flooded into the bottom of the building was acting like a gigantic fridge, cooling the whole place. Except for her torch the room was totally dark. This part of the hospital had no external windows – to maintain a sterile environment and to stop people from seeing in. What went on in operating suites was not for public viewing. Especially not today.

The door swung open and a girl came in with some blankets. She put one around the nurse's shoulders. It was blissful, like a hot bath. 'Thanks, Vicky,' the nurse said. Her rhythm squeezing on the bottle never faltered. Squeeze – hiss. Squeeze – hiss. That was what was keeping the patient alive.

Vicky put the other blanket over the patient, careful not to disturb the drips that ran into his arm. She looked shell-shocked. Poor girl, thought the nurse, she had only just started work there that afternoon. So far she'd had a hell of a first day.

Vicky went back to the stores to collect some more blankets. She had two fleeces on under her scrubs but still she was freezing cold. The head torch cast weird shadows in the corners.

She had been looking forward to taking up her first hospital job after qualifying. She'd been a PA back home in Wales and had retrained as a hospital administrator. She'd never dreamed that her first day at work would be like this. It had started badly enough – she had been delayed on the train and had to come straight to the hospital, without stopping off at her flat first. She hadn't even sat down at her desk when the flood hit. She had still been trying to find her way around the computer system when the power failed. Everyone was calm and just waited for the generators in the basement to come on. Except that they didn't. And slowly the news had sunk in that they weren't going to start either – the building was surrounded by water and the level was rising.

Then all hell broke loose. Nurses burst out of the operating theatres calling for lights – and help. Vicky suddenly found herself in a darkened scrub room, along with every other nurse, porter and secretary. They were told to wash their hands and put on gloves and gowns. Vicky was given some head torches and instructed to take them into one of the operating theatres.

When she had put her head torch on and pushed open the theatre doors, the sight that greeted her was like something from a bad dream. Her light fell on the incision in the patient's side and she saw a mass of blood spilling over the green cloth and onto the floor below. Quickly she looked away, but immediately the surgeons yelled at her for directing the light away from their work. They hadn't spotted the bleeding until she came in with the torch. She'd had to stare at the spurting artery while they got to work with metal clamps. They couldn't waste precious seconds putting head torches on themselves; instead they made her stand over the table like a mobile spotlight.

Vicky began to make sense of the shape on the operating table in front of her. The wound was in the patient's hip. It was an appalling mess. The surgeons had been cutting muscle away, to get down to the bone to insert a replacement hip, but now they had to abandon the operation and just try to patch up the damage. Vicky wanted to be sick, but she didn't dare move – the surgeons were relying on her light to work on the patient.

Vicky was aware of the anaesthetist and a nurse at the patient's head and she suddenly had a terrible thought: what about the anaesthetic or whatever was keeping the patient asleep? Would that fail without the power?

The nurse finally grabbed a head torch from her and went hunting in the cabinets. She brought back a loaded syringe and injected it straight into the patient's drip.

Finally the surgeons got control of the bleeding and Vicky was allowed to move away and distribute the other torches.

When she stumbled out of the theatre, she felt sick to her stomach. As she struggled to calm herself down, she told herself she was lucky. She could have been down in casualty or outpatients, or working in the morgue. They had been completely flooded. No one knew what had happened to the patients and staff there.

One by one, the patients in the theatres were closed up and wheeled out. Their operations would have to be performed again later. All the surgeons could do was sew up cut vessels, repair the holes they had made in muscles, stitch together the skin.

Now each of those patients lay in a recovery room, a theatre nurse standing over them, checking their progress. One of them had stopped breathing after the operation, and had to be resuscitated by hand. A nurse was bending over him, squeezing a bag that pushed air in and out of his lungs.

When Vicky had visited operating suites before, they had been busy places, full of bustle and the background hum of machines. Machines that made a soft hissing as they breathed for the patient, bleeped quietly as they monitored heart and brain activity. There was none of that noise now; it was silent and eerie. The only sound was the rhythmic hiss of the ventilating bag.

As Vicky walked past another recovery room, she saw the nurse's head in a ghostly circle of light like a halo; she was checking the patient's pulse with a worried expression. The nurse saw her light and called out to her. 'Vicky, can you get Doctor Okanga to dispense me some more morphine? I think he's coming round.'

'Yeah, sure.'

She hurried along to the pharmacy. This was the moment she had been dreading. When the poor, hastily patched-up patients came back to consciousness.

And would they have to evacuate? If the flood waters rose any higher, would they have to move the patients elsewhere? Surely they could not stay in a hospital without power . . . ?

Chapter Twenty-one

Ben thumped hard against the door with his shoulder but the bolt was solid and it held. The sound reverberated around the cellar.

Was that another sound – something in the water? Not for the first time, he peered down into the gloom, trying to see how deep it was, But he couldn't see anything. The cellar was black.

He would have to try and take a run at the door. He stepped down gingerly, feeling his way with his feet. He'd have to be careful otherwise he'd fall down the stairs.

He launched himself up at the door and hit it with his shoulder.

It hardly moved.

Ben listened for a moment. Maybe the sound of him trying to break out would bring somebody. He shouted out.

Suddenly he heard a voice. No, it was only the radio, still broadcasting reassuring messages. The voice seemed to have been chosen specifically to sound authoritative and soothing, like a drug. *'This is the BBC, coming to you from our Manchester studios. All other services have been suspended after the flooding in the capital today. Scheduled programmes will be repeated at a future date. For details you can check our website, which we hope will be back on line shortly.'*

How absurd, thought Ben. Criminals might be roaming the streets of London, Big Ben might have stopped, but BBC Radio was thinking about an orderly future, with *The Archers* and *The Chart Show*.

He needed a longer run-up. He turned round, put his right shoulder against the wall and felt his way down the stairs very cautiously. One, two, three.

There was something on the fourth step; he tripped and lost his balance, stumbling into the dark. Horrible images flashed through his head – stories about people falling to their deaths down cellar steps. He crashed onto his shoulder and rolled on down. Instinct made him tuck his head in, protect it at all costs.

He was suddenly engulfed in freezing water. He cried out and his mouth filled with that same foul taste he'd choked out earlier that day. He flailed around, as if trying to wake from a nightmare. Then his feet found solid ground.

He stood up and started for where he thought the stairs were, but then realized he hadn't a clue what direction to take.

Deep breaths, he told himself. *Panicking will definitely get you drowned.*

The water was up past his waist here. It chilled him to the bone. Where had it all come from?

This street wasn't underwater – the flood started at least a street away – it must be seeping through the ground, through the basement levels. Perhaps through a drain or an underground river. He forced himself to be calm. He needed to be able to see where he was going. In a moment his eyes would adjust.

Ben's patience paid off. He saw a gleam of light and waded over to it.

He came up against a wall, but at his eye level there was a hole. When he looked through, he saw a crawl space under the floor above, and daylight.

So the cellar didn't go the full length of the building. He saw a bank of bare earth and foundations like rough brick pillars resting on them. There was light coming through – enough for him to see the wood grain of the floorboards of the ground floor above. It smelled dank and rotten. There seemed to be debris in there too – crisp packets and polystyrene burger boxes – but that was a good sign: it must have blown in from the outside. And that definitely meant a hole. The space itself looked tight, but he reckoned he could crawl through.

Ben realized that, in the time he'd been standing there, the water level in the cellar had risen. It was now nearly up to his armpits.

No time to waste, then. He put his hands on the

rough brick sill of the crawl space and hoisted himself up. With so much buoyancy from the water it was easy, like vaulting out of a swimming pool. He wriggled into the space on his stomach, then pulled himself along on his elbows. It was cramped, like crawling under a bed, but not too bad if you kept your eyes on the light.

A squeaking, skittering sound made him start in alarm. He recoiled and banged the back of his head on wooden floorboards.

Something was in there with him.

Suddenly Ben could see small points of light, like sequins. They flashed at him, then moved away.

What were they?

Something brushed past his arm and he heard the squeaking again. This time he saw more sequins of light, some of them blinking at him. Then he saw torpedo shapes running about, then stopping abruptly. Tails flicked in the gloom.

The crawl space was full of rats.

Ben went cold all over. What was this under his hands? It felt like earth, but was it rat droppings?

He felt bile rising in his throat. He wanted to turn

round and go back there and then. But this was the only way out of the cellar.

All at once Ben felt a sense of hopelessness rising in him. He cursed Bel, wished she could see what he was having to go through because she'd mucked him about. He'd certainly give her all the horrid details. No, that would be pointless. She would probably say she'd had to do worse before her press conference after the tsunami in Phuket, or something similarly unsympathetic.

Ben realized he'd already battled against worse today, when he slipped off the raft into the water. This wasn't nearly as hard; just disgusting. He had to just pick a goal and work towards it.

The opening had a pattern over it, like some kind of mesh. More importantly, it was ten metres – four brick pillars – away. He kept his eyes on that light, and pulled himself along with his elbows.

Tiny squeaks and squeals flitted at the corner of his consciousness. Clawed feet ran across his bare hands. Scaly tails lashed his face. They touched his lips and he spat them out, swearing, trying not to think what would happen if the rats bit him.

He passed one brick pillar. Good. That was a land-mark.

A furry body brushed against his nose, filling his senses with the smell of wet rodent. Despite his resolve, he almost turned round, only there wasn't room.

That was when he started to realize how tiny the space was. The floorboards above, the pillars of brick to the side, the earth under his belly. He might get stuck here and die. Die, and be food for the rats.

He passed another brick pillar. The ground was getting wetter, slimier. Obviously the rain was coming in, but that was a good sign: it meant he was getting closer to outside.

The tiny eyes watched him as the rats skittered to and fro across his path. *Look all you want*, he thought. *Soon I'm going to be out of here.*

Slowly Ben passed the third pillar. Daylight was just a few metres away. Unfortunately, in front of him he saw a mass of small brown bodies. They stopped and looked at him: tails, ears, rodent faces. For some reason these rats didn't run away. It was like they knew they didn't have to be afraid of him: he was in their underworld and was vastly outnumbered. He saw their teeth and had a vision of them swarming towards him, to pick his bones clean.

Well, they'd have to get through his jeans first. And a rather expensive Burberry mac.

Then suddenly, as Ben focused on the opening ahead, he saw what it was, and all the fight went out of him.

It was merely a row of air bricks, designed to ventilate the underside of the building. From a distance it looked like a big hole with a mesh like a radiator cover, but up close it was solid bricks with a honeycomb pattern. There was no big hole.

The rats scurried around him, squeaking. Two of them sniffed at his hands. He struggled not to shake them off in case they bit him. Claws danced across his legs, his back.

Now what could he do? He was stuck under a building, in a stinking den of rats.

He'd have to go back.

With difficulty he turned round, squirming like a snake, the rats finally scattering out of his way. He'd have to try the cellar door again, he thought, before the water level got any higher. Before the water level rose so high that it flooded the crawl space too.

Painfully Ben pulled himself back towards the cellar. He was heading into the dark, and now his night vision had been bleached away by the glimpse of daylight. He hoped his eyes would adjust by the time he got back to the cellar.

Long before he had expected to, his hand found the cellar wall. Oh well, that had gone much more quickly than the outward journey. He put his hands out, still unable to see. Where was the hole?

He felt along the wall. Where was it? He shifted his body to try and let the light from the airbricks past. A tail swished in front of his face. Where was the hole?

He saw more light over to the right-hand side. That wasn't the cellar but it was better than nothing. Maybe it was more airbricks.

He pulled himself over to them.

The ground was becoming slimy again. He stopped and thought for a moment. He'd gone round in a circle. It was the same airbricks he'd found before. There was the same damp patch with the marks where he'd turned round. Now he was losing his sense of direction.

The rain pattered on outside, mocking him, as if to say, *It's all out here, you just have to work out how to reach it.*

He let his head sink onto his forearms. What could he do now?

He might have stayed there and given up if the smell hadn't been so disgusting. He lifted his head again. *Think*, he told himself. *You've had a panic, but that's over now. There must be a way to get out.*

In the light from the airbricks Ben could see that his hands and the sleeves of the Burberry were caked in mud. Wet slimy mud and drier earth from the area nearer the cellar.

That set a spark off inside his head. The ground near the front of the building was wet. Near the back, the cellar entrance, it was dry. He could get back to the cellar wall if he kept feeling for dry ground.

He squirmed round again. He felt a rat's whiskers tickling his cheek, its body solid, like a furry tennis ball. He tried to ignore it and concentrate on the task at hand.

He would do this systematically. He would pull himself forwards on his elbows, then check the ground. One pull, then he checked. Yes, it was drier. Another pull forwards. A burger wrapper stuck to his hands. He shook it off and scrunched it into a ball, then felt the ground. Dry. He was going in the right direction. Now he was using his brains: he was going to beat this.

It was then that Ben noticed the light coming from the right-hand side. It was fainter than the light from the air brick at the front, which was probably why he hadn't seen it before now.

He weighed up the options. Light was more promising than no light. He squirmed over to it.

It was a hole – a round tunnel of some kind like a sewage pipe, with a smooth inner surface, but big enough to get his shoulders into. Which meant the rest of him would go in too. The light wasn't directly ahead but reflecting off the wet inner surface of the tunnel. Several rats came down it, their claws skittering on the surface. He waved his arms and they turned and shot away, back the way they came.

Why hadn't he thought about that before? The rats

must have found a way in somehow, and they couldn't have come through the airbricks.

He squeezed into the space. A purple cable ran along one side. After the dank squalor of the crawl space the purple plastic was a reassuring connection with the civilized world. The light was dim but definite, and such a relief.

Ben noticed that the bottom of the pipe was covered in a thin sheen of mud. More rats came along and sniffed at his fingers and then his face. He didn't want to open his mouth with them so close so he blew out through his teeth at them and made a strange humming noise to scare them away.

His elbows began to feel tighter against his sides. His shoulders too. He had to hunch his head down more.

The space seemed to be getting smaller, or was it his imagination? Would it get too small for him? Would he get stuck in the tunnel?

Maybe he should have gone out through the cellar. Now he might not be able to get back at all.

Suddenly a breeze of fresh air stirred Ben's hair. Water was trickling down the tunnel, making a pattern in the silt along the bottom. It must be coming from outside. And it was definitely lighter or he wouldn't have been able to see that. He must be nearly out.

He felt air move above his head again. Cautiously he looking up, fearful of banging into the roof.

Then he realized there *was* no roof. Above his head was rain and air. He could see the sky and scaffolding. He was in a building site.

But it wasn't a way out. The hole in the tunnel was only about twenty centimetres long, not nearly big enough to get through. The tunnel was composed of half-cylinder sections and one of them had been lifted so that the cables could be fed in.

Ben pushed at the other segments but they were securely cemented in place and he couldn't get enough leverage to move them. He called out. His cries rang around the walls but no one came. All he could do was look at the big empty space above him and feel the rain on his face, as if he was stuck in a bizarre open coffin.

Chapter Twenty-two

The policeman was on his way back to the entrance of St Paul's Cathedral, carrying cups of tea for himself and Canon Victor Dibben. Out in the streets, car alarms and burglar alarms sang. A double-decker bus stood at the top of Ludgate Hill, abandoned. A few metres away, the river lapped at the bottom steps. St Paul's was on a hill and had just escaped the flooding. Now it was full of people taking refuge inside.

As the policeman rounded the corner and started up the steps, he saw that the Canon was speaking to a man outside the entrance.

'Come inside,' he was urging him. 'It's warm.'

'I don't need to come in,' said the man in a Spanish accent. 'I just need to get to Charing Cross Station. Where is it, please?'

It was more than an hour since Rebro had shut down and the policeman's radio was no longer functioning. The CCTV cameras in the area would have lost power long ago. Moreover, he'd lost his partner. He felt very alone.

Especially now – for he suddenly realized that there was something very strange about that man asking Canon Dibben for directions.

His hands were thrust deep into the pockets of his checked coat, and he looked as if he must have been walking for a long time: his black hair was plastered against his head, his clothes soaked.

Nothing unusual about that – so what was it that was making the policeman's instincts prickle?

From the interior of the great building came the sound of several hundred people, talking softly, moving around. Crowds of them had come in to shelter from the rain, but this man was asking for directions to Charing Cross Station. Was that what was odd, that he preferred to remain outside?

Everyone else who had staggered up the steps had been exhausted, seeking only warmth and something to eat.

Then it hit him – and he automatically tried to contact his station on the radio before he remembered he couldn't: it wasn't working. He was sure that a picture of the man the Canon was talking had been circulated around the stations that morning. He was José Xavier, a Basque separatist terrorist who had been arrested last night along with his accomplice, Francisco Gomez. The two of them had been taken to separate police stations to await transfer to the high-security station in Paddington Green for questioning.

But if it was indeed Xavier, where were his hand-cuffs? Maybe he had escaped before they had managed to cuff him.

The policeman decided to stay out of sight and went back down the steps. If the terrorist saw his uniform, Canon Dibben might be put in danger.

The Canon was still talking to the terrorist. 'We have hot tea and biscuits inside,' he told him. 'Are you sure you won't have some? You must be exhausted.'

The terrorist did look for a moment as though the

thought of food might tempt him in. *Go on, José,* the policeman willed him. *You need food. Have some food. Then I've got you.*

But Xavier moved away into the rain. As soon as he left, the policeman hurried up to the entrance, thrust both polystyrene cups into the hands of the Canon, then turned up the collar of his black raincoat. 'You'd better go inside,' he said to him. 'I'll see you later.'

'Where are you going?'

'I have to make an arrest.'

The policeman set off into the rain. He knew he couldn't let José Xavier walk away. The man was a dangerous terrorist. He had helped plant a car bomb in Madrid that had injured 65 people. If he let him go free, he might be a danger to other members of the public.

The policeman followed the terrorist down a small side street, unhooking the cuffs from his belt as he did so and checking they were open so he could snap them on quickly. He jogged along until he was close behind the check-coated figure. If he acted quickly, surprise would give him the advantage. The terrorist wouldn't expect to be spotted here.

'Excuse me, sir.'

The terrorist turned round. The policeman's hand was on the cuffs, ready to snap them onto the man's wrist. He grabbed his arm and started to twist it up into an immobilizing position.

Just as he noticed that the man was already wearing handcuffs, though obviously split apart, he felt a red-hot pain in his stomach.

He saw the glint of the blade as it flashed out of his abdomen, his blood smearing the bright steel with red. As the blade came towards him again, he tried to fend it off with his hands, but he was already growing weak and his reactions were sluggish. As the blade went in once more, his entire body was filled with pain and his legs buckled.

José Xavier watched the policeman crumple to the ground, the handcuffs dangling uselessly from his fingers. His blood pooled on the wet pavement though the relentless rain was already hosing it away. The policeman's eyes didn't seem to register him any more, they were completely fixed on his internal world of pain.

José looked around. No one had seen the incident –

and anyway, in this flood nobody cared about anything but saving their own skin. He bent down and shook the policeman's arm until he released the handcuffs. Then he pulled off the policeman's black waterproof coat and swapped it for his own, throwing the checked coat he'd been wearing over the policeman to hide the spreading pool of blood.

José picked up the policeman's hat, then turned his back on the huddled shape and continued on his way.

He had a rendezvous to make at Charing Cross.

'General Chambers, I've had a report about the Prime Minister.' The RAF corporal turned away from her desk to address him.

The General and the Chief Commissioner had been studying a map of the flood zone that Meena Chohan had helped to compile, but hearing the corporal's news the General went straight over to her workstation. 'And?'

The corporal took her headset off. 'It's not conclusive news, I'm afraid, sir. His staff say he was going to Gleneagles to play golf. His security filed the flightplan as per normal procedures and are going to get back to us with his exact position.'

The General let out a long, frustrated noise. He had prepared a briefing dossier to bring the Prime Minister up-to-date on what had happened and it had to be delivered as soon as possible. 'So he could be any-where between here and Scotland?'

'That's right, sir. But we should soon know exactly where he is.'

The General crossed to the controller, whose screen was showing a map of all the rescue helicopters and where they were. 'I want one of those helis standing by to go to the PM as soon as his location is confirmed. Top priority.'

Meena looked down at the reflection of the Puma in the water. They were over Epping Forest, but now the tops of the trees below looked like a paddy field. She wondered what her home near Chelmsford would look like now. Well, not long and she would find out.

'Hey, Dorek? Do you think you could drop me at Brentwood playing fields? I've missed my lift home with Mike from the Flying Eye.'

Dorek made a minute course correction. 'Don't see why not.'

Meena smiled. 'Thanks. I'll mention you on the breakfast show tomorrow.' She'd said it automatically, then caught herself. 'If there is a breakfast show tomorrow . . .'

A voice came through on Dorek's headset; he listened to it for a moment, then stated his position. 'Just passing over Epping Forest.'

The voice squawked in Dorek's headset for a moment, then he replied, 'Roger,' and changed course again. The helicopter swung around in a big circle and began to head back the way it had come.

'What's going on?' said Meena. 'Why are we going back?'

'Sorry, Meena, you won't be going home for a while. This takes priority. We've got to go see someone.'

Chapter Twenty-three

Ben lay in the pipe and let his forehead rest on the rough concrete. He was exhausted. He'd had enough. He just wanted to tune out the world and go to sleep.

The rain pattered onto the back of his head. It felt pleasantly cool. He hadn't realized how hot he was getting, inching along in the confined space. His shoulders, knees and elbows were sore from the friction. As he looked at the concrete pipe, the water trickling down the silt in the middle, he imagined pulling himself along on raw elbows again.

Perhaps he should just wait there until someone

came to the building site. At least he could breathe: he wasn't going to suffocate.

Even Bel might give up in a situation like this. Especially if there wasn't a camera to see it. She'd probably turn over and have a snooze, and then, when rescuers pulled her out, she'd be berating the government for allowing concrete to be used in construction, because it cost so much energy to produce and contributed to – you guessed it – global warming.

Ben shivered. He was cold again now. He'd have to get going again or he'd freeze. The purple cable snaked on into the distance. It had to lead somewhere. He just had to hope it was somewhere he could go too.

He started to inch down the tunnel again. His elbows, knees and feet were sore and his breathing was loud in his ears, echoing off the walls. In the confined space he could smell his own sweat and his clothes, which reeked of rat.

He started to think of his unpleasant Tube journey that morning, crowded in with people smelling wet and sweaty, water dripping off their umbrellas. He thought that had been unpleasant enough, with the wet seats and stale tunnel air, but compared with where he was now it was luxury.

He went on and realized that the tunnel was getting darker. Should he stop and turn back? He could barely see his hands in front of him on the ground now.

But he could smell something. He was no longer imagining being in the Tube; surely this *was* the Tube.

Suddenly his elbows had more room to move. Much more room. There was a big space beside him. He explored it with his hands. It was big enough to squeeze out of.

Ben felt almost dizzy with relief.

He pulled himself out and his hands met sharp items on a wet floor. As he brushed them aside, they made a metallic noise and one of them gave off a faint glint of light. But where was the light coming from?

In a wall high above Ben's head he saw a row of narrow slits. In front of him he could make out an open tool box, with wire cutters, spanners and screwdrivers strewn around the floor. That was what he had felt. In the wall was a cable conduit, its cover off.

Ben stayed on his hands and knees for a moment,

taking in deep breaths. He had done it: he had got out of the tunnel.

The smell of the Tube was really strong now, not just a faint odour stirring the memory, and he saw that the toolbox had a logo on it: London Underground. He must be in a station. The slits above him must be one of those ventilation shafts he had seen on the roofs of station buildings.

As he got to his feet, he realized he was in a tall room and below him he could hear a watery sound, like an open well. Nearby was a sign pointing to a staircase. He went over to have a look and saw that it led down into the dark depths. The slits of light in the roof above reflected down there as if in a mirror. The well was filled with water. Shapes floated there motionless, the water almost covering them like varnish. It was a few moments before Ben realized what they were: heads, backs, hands, a sodden base-ball jacket, a hoodie, a Drizabone hat. An iPod floating like a white tentacled thing in the water. Bodies.

He moved away quickly, and saw, on the other side of the room, a heavy dark wood door. It was open. On the floor by the toolbox was a torch. He picked it up and flicked it on, being sure to point it away from the bodies floating in the stairwell, then went through the door.

He found himself in a corridor. At the end an open door led to the booking concourse, where a sign said WELCOME TO HYDE PARK CORNER.

On the back of a chair beside the ticket barriers Ben spotted a navy blue jacket with LONDON UNDER-GROUND on it. He shrugged off the mac and put on the jacket instead. At least it was warm and dry.

Then he picked an exit from the concourse and went up to street level.

He found himself on an enormous traffic island. He'd almost hoped that the scene would have changed when he got out, but it was the same desolation he'd left behind when he'd gone into the sculptor's studio in Belgravia. Car and burglar alarms still shrieked alongside the seagulls and the rain came down relentlessly. You didn't need a compass to work out where the water was; you could see the cluster of helicopters hovering over it like birds of prey. Buses and coaches stood abandoned all round the island, and ducks, geese and swans from the royal parks still patrolled the puddles. Manhole covers lay on the tarmac, water bubbling up onto the road as though from some cauldron below. It stank of sewage.

But it wasn't a bad vantage point. The land sloped down towards Buckingham Palace to the south; it was surrounded by the dark lip of the water. If he remembered right, Charing Cross was near the river. All he had to do was follow the edge of the flood water eastwards.

As Ben turned his collar up against the unforgiving rain, he was back in the same miserable rhythm, one foot in front of the other. It was almost as if he had never strayed into the studio; as if he'd just been walking the whole time and imagined the whole bizarre incident. He was hungry and cold. If he kept moving, he thought, surely he'd get warm.

The image of the bodies in the Tube station followed him like a ghost, sending shudders through his rain-soaked skin. He began to think how lucky he'd been. What time had he come out of the Tube at Waterloo? And when had the flood hit? His train into London had been delayed. It could so easily have been delayed longer. He could have been trapped in the Tube himself. How many people were cocooned in that black water?

He reached Green Park Station and smelled that stale wet Tube station smell like the breath of old drains, heard the slap of water on shaft walls; saw in his mind's eye the bodies, hanging like discarded wetsuits in a dripping stairwell.

He passed the Ritz and glanced down a side street. He realized that he needed to keep closer to the edge of the water and went down a narrow street – one car wide and lined with very old, expensive-looking shops: a tailor with gold lettering on the window; a tobacconist with a dark oak humidifier, cigars laid out inside it like a bizarre delicatessen counter.

As he made his way south-east, Ben looked down the next street and realized it was flooded. He stopped and thought. Maybe he should turn back.

A figure was walking further down the street, his green gum boots splashing through the filthy water. The water was moving, as though it still carried the ferocious current of the Thames like an electric charge, but it didn't seem to be causing him any trouble.

Ben stepped in cautiously and carried on, past a wine shop displaying a dusty bottle of champagne as big as a traffic cone. He was so wet anyway, he didn't notice any difference between walking on dry land and wading. When he got to the end of the street he could head back up to the main road.

Ben had nearly caught up with the figure in wellies. 'Hi there,' he called out, but then the man took a step and vanished.

It was as if the ground had swallowed him.

Chapter Twenty-four

Ben froze. The man must have stepped into an open manhole. Stepped into it and gone straight down.

Ben searched the surface of the water. It swirled around his feet, a parked van, the lampposts, the bollards. There was no sign of the figure he had just seen walking along just moments before. No bubbles, no splashing; nothing rising to the surface. Not even a change in the swirl of the water to show where that manhole waited like an open mouth.

'Hello?' called Ben. There was no sound, just the ripple of moving water, claiming the city as its own. Ben's skin prickled colder and colder. He remembered being in the pipe, the feel of its walls pinning his arms in. A drain probably wasn't much bigger. You couldn't move your arms to keep yourself afloat. You'd go down like a stone. Then be swept away? What a horrible way to die.

It was like the city was a monster turning on its people.

And where was the drain? If he couldn't see it, how would he avoid it? He'd run back the way he'd come.

No, he couldn't, he thought. There might be open manholes there as well. He would reach dry land faster if he carried on to the end of the street than if he went back. Statistically there would be fewer manholes that way too.

OK: start walking.

Ben's body wouldn't obey him. He couldn't just play a game of Russian roulette and hope he wouldn't hit the unlucky spot.

There had to be a way to see them. Was there anything he could use as a guide? And where had the man disappeared? In the middle of the road? In the gutter?

He didn't know. It had happened so fast.

Ben shivered. He had been standing motionless and

was getting cold again. He had to get moving. He moved one foot forwards, keeping his weight on his back foot, and tested the ground ahead carefully.

The ground underneath seemed stable. He stepped forward and transferred his weight, then put the other foot forward and tested the ground again. So far so good. He was reminded of films he'd seen of people walking through minefields. He just had to keep his head, be sensible and not rush. That man had disappeared, straight down, in the time it took to blink an eye. Ben just had to take it one step at a time. Foot forward, test, transfer the weight. Repeat again, slowly. No rush.

The end of the road was coming steadily closer. Was he at the point where the man had disappeared?

Ben wished he hadn't thought of that. Somewhere, not far from where his feet were slowly passing, a man had lost his life. His body was probably still warm.

Once Ben's imagination started, it wouldn't stop. Once again he saw the bodies floating in the stairwell at Hyde Park Corner, the heads drooping, the shoulders rounded. He imagined the man with his head bowed like that in the narrow pipe.

Get a grip, he told himself. *It's not far now*. One step, then another. Soon he would be at the edge. Another step. He just had to take it slowly. He had come this far safely.

Carefully he felt around with his front foot – and this time it carried on down.

He stumbled backwards. There was open space beneath that foot and he'd nearly put his whole weight on it. He froze, his body shaking. He looked at the carpet of grey-brown water and saw a mass of hidden traps.

Helicopters were still buzzing over the water. He'd tuned them out, tuned out the alarms still calling to the wet sky, tuned out everything but his own footsteps. Now the noise clamoured in his ears, stopped him thinking.

He looked up at them. If he waved hard enough, would they swoop down and pick him up? Anything to avoid this tortuous walk.

But of course they couldn't see him, or if they could, they probably thought he wasn't in immediate danger.

He had to carry on, but the manhole was in front of

him and he dreaded that awful sensation of his foot going down and down.

He moved across to the side. That was OK. Then he took another step to the side. Surely a manhole couldn't be wider than two strides across.

He stopped, trying to screw up the courage to go forwards. The end of the street was just twenty metres away and then there would be firm ground.

He felt with his foot. The ground was solid, so he transferred his weight onto it. An irrational surge of adrenaline fired through him, and before he realized what he was doing, his legs were pumping hard, running through the water. It was like a switch had flipped in his brain. Forget the softly-softly minefield approach: he just had to get out. He wasn't thinking, he was just running crazily.

He reached the dry road and fell forwards onto his knees, his lungs dragging in air.

Chapter Twenty-five

As José Xavier walked along, he saw that this part of town was full of signs for lawyers' offices and financial institutions, punctuated by the odd sandwich bar. He was hungry, desperately hungry.

Once he saw the sandwich shops, he couldn't stop thinking about food. All that time in the pouring rain had taken its toll and his body craved calories just to keep warm. He tried the doors but they had been locked up carefully. People in this part of London obviously didn't just abandon their premises.

Through the windows of a solicitor's office he could see a figure moving around inside – a bald man in a suit; no doubt one of the solicitors. He had a packet of Hobnobs beside him.

José stopped, transfixed by the sight of the biscuits. He wasn't even aware that he was staring until the man caught sight of him and beckoned to him frantically.

José walked in, careful to keep his policeman's raincoat buttoned up high, his eyes fixed on the biscuits.

The bald man pointed across to a figure lying on the floor. 'She's there,' he told José. 'We pulled her out of the basement when it flooded.'

A woman was stretched out on her back. Her clothes were soaked and her black tights had gaping holes in them. Her hair flowed over her face like seaweed. The carpet around her was sodden, as though she was bleeding river water. A man in half-moon glasses was kneeling over her, trying to give her the kiss of life.

'The police are here,' the bald man told him, and Half-moon Glasses sat back on his heels looking relieved.

José put his hand out to the man with the Hobnobs. 'Give me those,' he ordered.

The bald man handed the packet over. José wolfed four of them immediately. It was the first thing he'd eaten for hours. Better than what was on offer in Snow Hill police station.

The two men looked at him, amazed, as though they'd expected him to give them to the unconscious woman as some kind of miracle cure.

'She needs help,' said Half-moon Glasses. 'We can't get her to breathe.'

José glanced at the woman. Even from this distance her clothes smelled of sewage. A drain must have flooded into the building. Her skin looked pale and waxy and her lips were blue.

While he'd been taking this in José had eaten four more biscuits. The rain dripped off his uniform onto the floor.

'She looks dead,' said José. He wandered through to the kitchen and opened the fridge door. The light didn't come on – of course – but there was a packet of sandwiches in there from one of the upmarket shops he had passed on the way here. He tore the packet open and took an enormous bite.

The bald man followed him. 'Aren't you even going

to look at her?' he demanded. 'Can't you call for help on your radio?'

José straightened up and hit him around the mouth. The bald man crashed to the floor, letting out a grunt of surprise and pain.

In the other room, Half-moon Glasses froze where he was, still kneeling by the dead woman. His eyes were wide and horrified.

By the sink was a bottle of bleach with a trigger nozzle. José seized it and pointed the nozzle downwards at the bald man's face, like a gun. Just in case he was thinking about trying to stop him getting away.

The bald man understood. He stayed where he was, leaning up on one elbow, his other hand on his bleeding mouth, watching José.

José walked to the door.

Outside, the rain was still tipping down, splashing noisily off the road and the gutters. José put the bleach bottle in his pocket, turned up his collar and went out.

In a back street in Mayfair, Francisco Gomez walked into a repair garage. It was very upmarket – there were no oily patches on the forecourt, as if cleaners came and scrubbed them away every day. A Mini stood on the inspection ramp, where it had been abandoned in the middle of an MOT. It was rather a modest car for this part of town, Francisco thought, but he guessed the mechanics had taken the Mercs and Jags and scarpered when the disaster hit.

The station had one petrol pump. Excellent: he could help himself to a can while he was here. You never knew when it might come in useful. He pulled the petrol nozzle out of the holder and squeezed the trigger. Nothing happened. It was probably locked from some central control indoors.

He made his way across to the office. A puffy jacket like the top half of a Michelin man outfit lay abandoned on an office chair. Francisco shrugged off the sodden donkey jacket and put the puffy jacket on. The warmth cocooned his soaking skin.

Now to find the switch to release the petrol pumps.

He found it first go, under the cash register. He pressed it, but still nothing happened. Too bad.

The cash register wouldn't open either.

Next to it was a phone. He picked up the receiver, but there was no tone. The phones were still out. He'd done that in every shop he'd been into. Not that he wanted to call anyone: his partner would hardly have been allowed to keep his mobile. Still, it was reassuring to know that no one else was able to talk to each other either.

Francisco went through a doorway into the covered garage area and saw tools lying scattered all over the floor.

He bent down and picked up a tyre iron. That's what he had been looking for. He looked at the Mini on the ramp. It was a pity he couldn't get it down – he might have been able to get to Charing Cross a bit faster. He didn't want José to think he wasn't coming.

Chapter Twenty-six

Ben stumbled up to two guys at the door of a shop. 'Excuse me, is this the way to Charing Cross?' he asked them. His arms were huddled around his body and he jogged from one foot to another. He was so cold he didn't want to stand still for a moment.

One of the guys turned round and glared at him, a sledgehammer held threateningly over his shoulder. Ben thought he was going to attack him and staggered slowly backwards, as if there was a five-second delay between his brain deciding to move and his limbs managing to obey.

'Ha!' said one of the guys. 'You been drinking,

mate?' He pointed along the road. 'There's a pub up there if you want some more.'

Ben stared at them. His brain was racing with things to say but his lips wouldn't work: *I'm not drunk. I've never been drunk in my life. I'm thirteen. I'm not drunk, just cold.*

The man turned back to the shop door. A slender diamond necklace glinted in the window, arranged on a black velvet cushion. 'Give it a good blow here, down in the corner,' said his friend. 'They build them with a weak spot so the Fire Brigade can get in.'

His partner aimed the sledgehammer carefully, then whacked the window hard. It disintegrated in a shower of glass. The looters let out a whoop of joy and hurried in, their feet crunching on the glass.

Ben stumbled on. The water was almost up to the main road, and quite deep in the side streets. One block over, a Smartcar glided past in the water, swept along like a paper boat. It caught against a bollard with a metallic thud. Something was moving inside: behind the windscreen he could see a face, the mouth making an O of a scream. It was a little girl in pigtails and a pink shirt. She saw him and waved frantically.

Then the car started moving again, the insistent current pulling it free, taking its helpless passenger with it.

He staggered back down the road: the man with the sledgehammer, he thought. If only he could find him, maybe he could smash open the window and let her out.

He stopped, realizing that it was too late – the car was gone now; they couldn't reach it. He just had to let go, accept there was nothing he could do.

He turned round and set off again, but all he could think about was that child's face, her pigtails shaking as she called out to him. She had seen him and thought he could help. Now what would happen to her? He felt responsible.

A little further along he saw a shape at the water's edge; it was catching on the road and then pulling away again with the rhythm of the tide slapping on the tarmac. He ran across to it. If he couldn't help the little girl in the Smartcar, maybe he could help here.

A cloud of seagulls rose as he approached. Seagulls, the new predators in this drowned city. Ben saw that it was the body of a dead man; the seagulls were checking it out as a source of food.

The body was wrapped in plain cotton material that clung to the skin. Underneath was a hospital gown. It was very still, like a lump of lard. Ben looked at it, puzzled. The eyes were closed and the face peaceful, as if the man had died in his sleep. On his arms were strips of tape, the loose ends floating on the water like seaweed, and tiny holes like needle marks. He had died in hospital, Ben realized. But how had he got out here? Had the river washed out the hospital mortuaries?

Ben backed away and the seagulls moved back in.

He stumbled on. He was so cold. Maybe it was because he was shocked. He kept thinking about the child in the Smartcar and the body in the sheet. Maybe he'd end up like that – a lump lying in the river surrounded by seagulls. He passed a man lying in a doorway, his teeth chattering like castanets, his body jerking violently. Maybe he should sit down for a while too, rest so that he could get his strength back.

No sooner had he thought it than he was on his knees in a shop doorway. Maybe he could just close his eyes for a minute. When he tried that, it felt so good. He wasn't aware of the hard edge of the door frame behind his back. It just felt so great to stop . . .

'Sir? There's a call for you from the Admiralty in High Wycombe. Top priority.' The controller at Hendon handed the satellite phone over to General Chambers.

The General took the phone to a quiet corner of the room. 'Chambers here.'

The voice at the other end of the phone sounded furious, and as though it was barely keeping that fury in check. 'General, make sure your men stick to communications protocols on the satellites.'

The General felt his hackles rise. 'They have been.'

'Well, someone's used a restricted channel and blocked the routine signal. We've got a Vanguard submarine that's missed its routine all-clear signal.'

The General went white. The buzz of the communications room around him disappeared for a moment as he took in what that meant. When he next spoke, his voice hissed quietly. 'My men have not breached protocols. The mistake didn't happen here.'

The voice at the other end didn't even seem to hear

him. 'Just keep your men off the restricted channels. And tell Whitehall they've got a situation.'

The faces of the sub crew looked haggard in the red light. The helmsman spoke. 'We're on the surface, Captain.'

'Radio mast is deployed and ready, sir,' said the communications officer.

'Very good,' said the captain. 'Communications officer, send your message.'

There had been no answer to the first message the sub had sent to Whitehall. Now they were repeating the procedure.

Once again, the communications officer watched the display. 'Message has been successfully sent, sir.'

The captain nodded. 'Helmsman, take us down.'

The helmsman was ready, his hands on the controls. 'Diving now, sir.' He watched the digital depth read-out as the sub once again submerged.

The first officer voiced his concerns. 'Captain, what do you think has really happened to London? This flood business is rather strange.'

The captain eased a crick in his neck. It had already

been a long day. 'You want the simplest explanation? For some reason the satellite wasn't working – maybe because of the flood. But someone's head needs to roll for that. Or maybe all this flood business is just a ploy by High Command to have an excuse to open fire. If it's a SNAFU, there are safeguards in the system to stop it escalating. In the meantime, we have our orders and it's our job to follow them. I'm going to talk to the crew.'

He unhooked the intercom. 'Gentlemen, we have attempted to communicate with Whitehall for a second time, and once again have exposed our position. It is possible that we may encounter enemy action. It is the job of everyone to stay vigilant. This is not an exercise.'

Chapter Twenty-seven

The Puma had flown due west, skirting over the top arc of the M25 and out over Buckinghamshire. They were flying higher than before, and faster. At that height, Meena couldn't make out the details she was used to seeing. The rusty-looking sprawl of London thinned out. The features of the landscape looked tiny, the different colour corduroy fields looking like a patchwork counterpane. But lakes of pale grey water still reflected in the sky and rivers showed up wide and swollen. Some houses were surrounded. Even out here, miles from the Thames, rivers had burst their banks and were trying to claim the land.

At least the traffic Meena saw was moving. Vehicle headlights trundled along the tiny lanes. But they were the only lights visible. There was not a single light in any of the buildings.

The Puma circled and hovered, then descended. Meena saw sprawling slate roofs with old-fashioned chimneys and windows. Tiny leaded panes of glass reflected the Puma's glittering lights. Then trees got in the way and the Puma touched down on a large letter H painted on a stretch of tarmac. It looked like they had landed in an expensive country hotel.

The whine of the engine diminished and the rotors wound down. A military tanker painted dark green drove out to meet them.

Dorek took off his helmet. 'Refuelling stop. No smoking.'

Meena and Phil unbuckled their harnesses and made to get out.

'No time for that,' said Dorek.

The refuelling crew was already starting work. Meena felt a couple of metallic bumps as the fuel cap was unscrewed, then a humming reverberated through the fuselage. She realized it was the tanker delivering fuel.

She looked out of the window in dismay, then back at Dorek. 'You mean they're refuelling with us on board?'

'That's nice,' said Phil. 'What if it catches fire while we're in here?'

'Don't be an ass,' said Dorek. 'What if it drops out of the sky when we're five hundred feet up?'

Meena had to quell her worries. Normally on civilian planes you didn't refuel when there were people on board. Sitting there while the fuel pulsed into the tank felt wrong, but she had to accept that the army did things differently. And she didn't want to appear a wimp.

A soldier stepped up to Dorek's window and handed him another laptop. 'General Chambers says the briefing documents are all on there.'

The ground crew had nearly finished refuelling. Meena looked out of the window and saw, over the trees, an Elizabethan mansion, like a hotel. 'Er – where exactly are we?'

'Chequers.'

Meena thought she'd misheard. 'Chequers? As in where the Prime Minister lives?'

'Yep,' said Dorek. 'We've got to go take him some homework.'

No, go away, thought Ben. *Leave me alone. I want to sleep.*

'Wake up,' a voice was shouting. 'You've got to wake up.'

Hands grasped his shoulders and shook him. Ben tried to bat them off. He turned over, trying to retreat into his cocoon of sleep. When he moved, rain trickled down inside the collar of his jacket.

Still the hands shook him. 'Wake up. You can't sleep.' Something was touched to his lips. 'Drink this.'

He tasted warm Coca-Cola. It went down the wrong way, and he coughed and sat up. Water streamed down his forehead. *Go away*, he thought.

'Are you awake?'

He forced his eyes open and saw a tubby girl wearing a black zip-up jumpsuit and a neoprene balaclava. For a moment he thought he'd been kidnapped by aliens. Except for her red lipstick and her eye make-up running in the rain.

'Who are you?' he said.

'Eva.' She held out a Mars Bar. 'Eat this – it'll give you energy.'

Ben suddenly realized he was ravenous. He snatched the Mars Bar but could barely tear open the wrapper. His fingers felt like fat sausages, all boneless and uncontrollable. Eva had to open it for him. He wolfed the bar down in three bites.

She handed him the Coke can again. 'Have some more.'

He drank it obediently.

The sugar rush started immediately, as if it had been injected directly into his veins. He started to shiver.

Eva pulled him to his feet. 'Come on, we'd better get you something warm.'

He still didn't want to move; he felt too cold for that. He wanted to curl up in a ball so that he could keep warm.

Eva linked her arm through his and nudged his legs with his feet. 'Come on, start walking. You're getting hypothermia – that's why you don't want to move. But if you stay in that doorway you'll die.'

Ben groaned.

'Come on,' said Eva, and shook him. 'Once you get moving you'll feel better.'

Ben started to walk, leaning heavily on her. It wasn't her words that made him try; it was her running eye make-up. It made her look like Marilyn Manson. He wasn't going to disobey someone who looked like that.

They were approaching a big interchange. Large, old-looking buildings surrounded a statue of some guy with wings. Buses stood abandoned and the road was littered with debris.

Ben realized he knew the place. 'Is this Piccadilly Circus?'

'Yeah,' said Eva.

Ben clung onto Eva's arm as she led him purposefully across the road. He remembered Piccadilly Circus as a crowded, bustling place. Now the huge advertising signs stood dark, brooding over the deserted roads. The giant record shop on the corner was no longer a vibrant place pumping out music. It was empty and silent.

Funny how those things still took Ben by surprise. He felt like any second he would wake up back in his bed in Macclesfield.

'In here,' said Eva. She pushed open a door.

Ben found himself surrounded by golf carts and checked trousers. They were in the sports store Lillywhites. And mercifully, it was dry.

'Up here,' said Eva. She dragged him towards the stairs.

Ben groaned again. Now that he'd stopped, he didn't want to move. 'Can't we use the lift?' he asked, before he realized it wouldn't be working.

'It's only three floors,' she said.

He followed Eva's jumpsuited rear, pulling himself up by the handrail. She had funny little boots too; they seemed to be part of the jumpsuit. Why was she dressed like a black Teletubby?

She waited for him by the fire doors at the top. He tried to push the door open but the spring was heavy and he had to give it a second go.

They emerged on the shop floor, in the diving department. Ben saw a chair and went to sit down.

'Don't sit down for a moment,' Eva ordered him. 'I need to see what size you are.'

Ben stopped where he was and looked at her

wearily. She looked him up and down. 'OK, now you can sit.'

Ben sank down on the chair while Eva marched off. Short-sleeved diving suits hung around him, crisscrossed with zips and smelling of rubber. He realized that was what Eva's weird outfit was: a diving suit.

She came marching back with a handful of multi-coloured items and dumped them in his lap. 'Eat those. And don't you dare go to sleep again.'

They were energy bars. Ben picked one up and pulled at the wrapper. His fingers were still cold and it was no easier to undo than the Mars Bar. How ironic, he thought, if you died because you didn't have the strength to open your energy bar. He put the wrapper between his teeth and tore it. He wolfed one bar down, then started on a second.

'You're not asleep, are you?' called Eva's voice. He couldn't see her between the racks but he could hear the scrape of hangers on rails.

'No,' called Ben, crumbs dropping out of his mouth.

'Get undressed.'

'Eh?' Ben stopped chewing for a moment, thinking he'd misheard. He swallowed. 'What?'

'Take your clothes off. You'll catch your death.'

'But—'

'Go on.' He heard more hangers squeak as Eva searched through them.

Her tone was so insistent Ben realized he'd have to comply. He didn't want that strange streaky face looming over him asking him if he was shy. He stood up and took off the London Underground jacket, then his sweatshirt. It was stuck to his arms and he had to practically peel it off. It fell in a filthy heap on the floor. He hadn't realized how disgusting it was until he saw it lying there. It looked like he'd crawled through a mud pit in it.

Eva came tramping back through the rails again. She dumped a pile of gear at his feet. Ben was about to take his T-shirt off, then stopped, embarrassed.

'Go on,' she said. 'I need to see how well co-ordinated you are.'

Ben pulled the T-shirt off over his head.

'You'll live.' Eva pointed at the clothes dumped on the carpet. 'See if any of those fit. I'll be back in a minute.'

He didn't touch them until she was well out of the way, swishing hangers again.

She'd brought packets of black thermal underwear. He ripped one open and his fingers felt the soft pile of the fabric. Just the touch of it made him feel warmer. He shook it out of its packet. It was a long-sleeved vest. He couldn't get into it fast enough. As his arms slid in he felt a huge sense of relief. His skin felt warm for the first time in hours.

Eva came back with a small black neoprene item.

Ben examined it cautiously. 'A hood?'

'You lose a lot of heat through your head,' said Eva. 'Put it on.'

There was a mirror nearby. He pulled the hood on and glanced at his reflection. Dirty, grime-smeared face, hollow eyes, purple lips all framed by a tight black hood. He looked like a nightmare.

Eva came back again with a black and grey jump-suit. It was stiff and long and practically stood up by itself.

'Hold this,' she told him.

Ben took it by the shoulders and she knelt down and started undoing zips in a workmanlike way.

It was a peculiar garment. It even had its own

boots, dangling off the end of the legs as if someone had welded a pair of wellingtons to it.

'Eva, what is it?'

'A drysuit.' She stood up. 'Put your leg in there.'

He did as he was told. He got one leg in and wiggled it down. It got stuck halfway.

'There's something inside,' he told her.

'It's this,' said Eva. She seized the knee pad and scrubbed the fabric together in her hands, like someone trying to open a stubborn plastic bag. 'Now push,' she said.

Ben got one leg in, then the other. But that wasn't all. Eva knelt down and did up a complicated system of zips around the legs. The suit got tighter and tighter.

'Now pull those elastic braces up over your shoulders.'

Ben took hold of a brace but the elastic was too tight. It twanged out of his hand and disappeared down the inside of the suit. He laughed.

Eva watched him without a flicker of a smile. 'A lot of people lark about when they put a drysuit on.'

'Sorry,' said Ben. He didn't think he'd ever come

across anyone so serious. He tried the braces again and didn't do any better the second time.

'You've got to pull hard. They're made to be tough.'

Finally he got them up and Eva zipped up the back of the suit. Now he was in.

He looked at her again, her Marilyn Manson face framed by the hood, and started to giggle. 'Now we both look like Teletubbies.'

Eva didn't think that was funny either. 'At least you've got your sense of humour back.' She said it with a completely straight face, as though she was a scientist observing an experiment.

Ben felt bad that he might have offended her. She had probably saved his life. 'Thanks' – he gestured at his strange outfit – 'thanks for all this.' He put out his hand. 'I'm Ben, by the way.'

Eva shook his hand solemnly. 'Well, Ben, if I hadn't come along, who knows what would have happened to you.'

'You seem to know a lot about all this.'

'I'm a qualified diver. We're taught to recognize the signs of hypothermia. Your body loses heat fast when you're wearing wet clothes. Then you start to go wrong, like an old machine. You can't think straight. You just want to lie down and sleep but that's the worst thing you can do because you lose heat even faster if you stop moving.'

She seemed to take a peculiar delight in describing these gloomy details. But Ben had to admit that, although she only looked a few years older than he was, she seemed to know her stuff; it was as though she'd been following him with a video camera.

'It's not nice, is it?' he said.

'No,' said Eva. 'I had it once while wreck-diving in Plymouth.' She started towards the exit. 'Come on.'

Ben followed her. It was only when he started to move that he realized there was a bulging seam that forced his legs apart like a bandy cowboy's. Even worse, his shins felt like they were being scraped raw.

He stopped. 'Eva, are you sure I've got this on properly? It hurts.'

Eva barely even glanced back at him. 'It's probably the lining. Those ones are a bit sticky at first if you haven't waxed your legs.'

Sticky wasn't the word for it. It was like every hair

was being pulled out of his skin. Still, it was better than that awful, creeping, deathly cold.

Ben passed another mirror and saw that the suit was light grey across the shoulders and black further down. In the middle of the chest was a valve with a yellow logo around it. There were curious pockets all over the place with nobbles and zips. He looked like Batman, especially with the hood. But he'd better not say so to Eva.

More seriously, though, he realized how much better he was feeling. He'd felt so cold and miserable before.

'Come on,' called Eva in a strict voice. 'You need more fluids.'

She was a bit of a bossy boots, thought Ben. Still, he was grateful for the company. And if she hadn't come along, he might still be in the doorway, sinking into oblivion.

Chapter Twenty-eight

Francisco reached Trafalgar Square. He entered at the top, by the columns of the National Gallery. The water lapped along the tarmac at the bottom edge. Nelson looked out sadly over the flood.

He walked past St Martin-in-the-Fields and saw the station on the other side of the road: Charing Cross.

But then he saw that the station was surrounded by water.

Still, water or not, he had to get in. At least that might mean he'd have the place to himself.

He crossed the road and got as close to the station as he could to assess the situation. The forecourt had an in-and-out drive, bounded by a set of iron railings. They would do.

He launched himself into the water. The current swept him along with surprising power, but Francisco had calculated well. He grabbed the railings. The current tried to pull him away and the tyre iron clipped to his belt dragged him down, but he clung on.

Without letting go, he put his feet down. The water was nearly up to his waist. Holding onto the railings, he began to work his way along. Each step he took, he felt with his feet first. He knew there could be dangers lurking in the water. He felt the smooth pavement under his feet change to the cobbles of the forecourt. He reached the end of the railings, where the exit to the forecourt was.

The station entrance was opposite him now, a series of arches about twenty metres away. It would be good if he could let go and the current could swoosh him through one of those arches like a football into a goal. But judging by the wrappers and rubbish swirling past him, it was running out into Trafalgar Square. If he tried to wade or swim, he would be swept away too.

However, at the end of the forecourt he spotted

some cars smashed up against a row of shops, piled up as if in a junkyard. He could use those as handholds.

Francisco reached out for a car on its back like an upturned beetle. His hands caught the filthy underside of its exhaust. It took his weight and he swung onto it, like Tarzan. The exhaust pipe ran up the entire underside of the car and he pulled himself along to the front bumper.

Next was a taxi, which had managed to remain upright. He used its wing mirror to reach the handle-bars of a Suzuki motorbike. Then he moved onto a police car: its open window provided a generous handhold. And then he was in the goalmouth.

It was also under water, but he felt smooth, level tiles under his feet. Within the station the current wasn't so bad and Francisco stopped to get his breath back.

From that vantage point he took stock. First he checked to make sure there was no one else around. It had become a habit, from long years of doing things and trying to avoid being seen. Right now, though, it would have been good to see his partner José but there was no sign of him. He might as well get on.

Francisco waded over to the red metal left luggage lockers. They'd chosen one on the third rack – at the time this was because it was the least visible to CCTV cameras, but now – luckily it also meant that the contents wouldn't be ruined.

Francisco's keys had been confiscated by the police when he was arrested. But it didn't matter; the tyre iron would do fine. He unhooked it from his belt and edged it into the gap beside the lock. It fitted perfectly.

He levered open the door and started to look through the contents. There was a rucksack and a couple of warm jackets. He threw off his Michelin top and let it float away while he put on one of the jackets from the locker. They were reversible: wear them one way round and they showed distinctive motor racing logos; the other side was a plain colour. That way, if they were spotted, the most likely thing that would be reported was the logo. All they had to do then was switch to the other side and they were incognito again.

The locker also contained a collection of Ordnance Survey maps. Francisco pulled out the ones for Berkshire and Oxfordshire and left the rest. Their best bet was to follow the Thames upstream and disappear into the countryside. He slipped the maps into plastic cases to protect them from the rain.

Next he found the first aid kit and a bottle of Evian water. He unscrewed the cap with his teeth, drank some, then pushed up the sleeves of his jacket and poured a little onto the wounds on his wrists where the handcuffs had been. They had been soaking in that filthy river water for ages and he didn't want them to go septic. Scabs had begun to form, so he picked them off. It was painful but bleeding was the most natural way to get all the rubbish out of the wounds. He sluiced water over them again, took some antibiotic cream out of the first aid kit and smeared it on. Then he fastened the first aid kit again and put that in the rucksack.

There were other things to pack too. Francisco found the bars of Kendal mint cake, pulled the wrapper off one and ate it there and then. A couple of torches with spare batteries. Bolt cutters; two compasses. A sheath knife; a serrated knife. A Second World War knuckleduster knife – an unexpected find while shopping in an army surplus store in north London. It had a vicious steel blade about sixteen centimetres long, and a brass handle in the shape of a knuckleduster; it was a fearsome-looking weapon. He slipped it into the inside pocket of his jacket.

Now he was getting to the bottom of the locker and pulled out a small attaché case. The case itself was shielded with metal so that if the contents of the locker were x-rayed they wouldn't show up. Francisco set the combination to the correct position and the lock sprang open. Inside was £1,000 in cash in a waterproof zip bag, along with some credit cards and fake passports – and a Beretta 7.6mm pistol. The pistol had been bought with cash from a friend of a friend. Francisco lifted it out of its casing and snapped the ammunition clip into the grip with the heel of his hand.

'Spare some change, guv'nor?'

Francisco whirled round, his heart thumping. A bedraggled-looking man with the corned-beef complexion of a down-and-out was standing looking at him, wearing the jacket he had discarded. He was also looking at the open locker with the gun case and the cash in the see-through bag.

You've seen too much, thought Francisco. He

pulled the trigger And the shot echoed around the walls. Pigeons fluttered in the rafters.

The tramp collapsed immediately, face down in the water. He drifted towards Francisco, who nudged him away with his leg. Blood spread out in a cloud from under the white jacket.

Yes, the gun worked fine.

Chapter Twenty-nine

'One of our submarines is on red alert because it has missed its routine all-clear signal. We are dealing with the situation – there's a Nimrod jet on its way out there – but we thought you needed to be informed.'

The Chief Commissioner and General Chambers watched the faces on the screen digest the news. They had called a meeting of all the senior personnel in the bunker. Civil servants from the Ministry of Defence were crowded into the briefing room, along with Sidney Cadogan and Clive Brooks from the Department of the Environment. The Foreign Secretary was there, and that noisy woman Bel Kelland was still there too.

Madeleine Harwood was the first to speak. She was furious. This had been the worst day of her life as a politician, ever. First she'd had to authorize the shutting down of Rebro, then give the go-ahead to the military to use whatever force necessary – including firearms – to deal with looters, and now it looked like she was having to deal with a potentially very serious international incident. As Foreign Secretary, however, this was clearly within her portfolio and she felt on firmer ground responding. 'It's ridiculous that in this day and age this sort of thing can happen,' she snapped. 'We have safeguards and protocols.'

General Chambers had expected something like this. That was why he and the Chief had set up their end of the link in a private office, away from the emergency control room.

'We do have protocols, ma'am,' he replied. 'They were set by Whitehall.'

Madeleine Harwood rounded on a woman sitting next to her with blue-rimmed glasses and a severe suit. 'I want an internal inquiry.'

'So do I,' snapped the woman. 'But until it makes its

report, I don't think you should be pointing the finger of blame.'

The General tried to bring the meeting back to the subject in hand. They could bicker all they wanted once he'd said what he needed to say, but if they did it now they were wasting precious satellite time.

The Chief Commissioner sat behind him, his arms folded, his head down. This meeting wasn't his territory; he was just an impartial observer.

'The situation is a cause for concern,' said General Chambers, 'but as long as the submarine follows its standing orders, it will get the message to stand down.'

Bel had been listening, her sharp chin resting on a folded arm. Now she sat up. 'So if one transistor fails somewhere – in the satellite or in the sub or at your end – we've got an international crisis. That's great.'

'Dr Kelland,' said the woman in the severe suit, 'there are a million failsafes in our systems. And I'd like to remind you this is classified information and—'

Bel shook her head, her pale blue eyes narrowed as she interrupted her. 'Don't you get it? One day it will fail. This flood has caused a million tiny bits of chaos today. Only one of them has to get out of control and who knows what might happen?'

General Chambers stood up and cut the video link. The screen went blank. 'We've done our bit. I think we can just leave them to it,' he told the Chief Commissioner.

Dorek took the Puma down low. Meena, resting her head against the window, saw fields rush up towards her, then a small town, its buildings and streets completely dark. Traffic crept along its roads like ants. Dorek took them in a quick circle, the Puma tilting at forty-five degrees, then rose nearly vertically.

Meena held onto her stomach. 'Dorek, do we have to do this? You're flying like a demented bee.'

'It's a search pattern,' he told her.

Meena leaned her head against the window again. Headphones snaked out from under her green helmet. Her mobile had a radio and she had found a programme that wasn't sending out emergency broadcasts. It was a phone-in programme in French, which she spoke fluently. It made peculiar listening.

The host was cajoling listeners to call in with their views on the topic of the day – which was the disaster in London. It seemed like the French public were letting their imaginations run riot.

'*What will happen to the stock market? New York and Tokyo won't have been able to do anything – the world economy will collapse. We should all be very worried about our pensions.*'

'*The stock market will be moved out of London to Paris,*' said another caller confidently.

Phil's voice on the headset inside the helmet drowned out the French scaremongering for a moment. 'Dorek, what's that down there? Circle around that traffic jam at eleven o'clock.'

Dorek nudged the stick and the Puma dropped its nose and swooped down like a bird. Meena felt queasy as the ground loomed up fast again.

Down below, a group of cars was clustered around a junction, vying for who would move first. Some people had got out and were having an argument. Wherever you went, it seemed people always had time for road rage.

'Just another set of broken lights,' said Meena.

Dorek swung upwards again, leaving them behind.

In her headphones, the French listeners were exploring another rich seam of woe. '*London has squandered our artistic heritage. It built its art galleries and museums too close to the river. Thousands of Europe's treasures will have been ruined. It's like New Orleans. When that flooded, the water was raw sewage. So all those ruined paintings can't be cleaned. They will have to be burned.*'

Meena was starting to find this irritating. This French programme seemed to be enjoying these terrible events. '*If this can happen to London,*' said a deep Gallic voice, '*what about the Netherlands? The Netherlands should be thinking about evacuating its people. For some countries this could be the end of civilization as they know it.*'

They sped away from the traffic jam and out over open fields. Then Meena saw barbed wire fences, green military vehicles and low buildings, with people in khaki uniforms moving between them. A military base. Parked on the asphalt at the front was a helicopter.

'That looks like our chap,' said Phil.

The helicopter's wings were hanging down, at rest.
A figure wearing khaki plus-fours was standing beside
it, under a striped golf umbrella, chatting to a couple
of soldiers.

Dorek circled the Puma around in a movement that
nearly had Meena depositing her breakfast out of the
window. He stopped and hovered.

The figure in plus-fours tilted the umbrella back
and looked up. Meena recognized him immediately: it
was the Prime Minister. Beside him, getting rather
wet, was his security guard; a tall, thickset guy in a
suit with a bulge like a holster under his arm.

The PM gave the Puma a cheery wave.

'*England is certainly finished*,' said the merry
people of France in Meena's headphones.

No we're not, she thought, and pulled the cables
out of her ears. She put her phone onto video mode.
There was just enough battery for a few exclusive
shots of the PM, safe and well and about to receive his
first briefing on the rescue operation.

Chapter Thirty

Ben had a torch in each hand. He switched them on and played them over the walls of the darkened stairwell. The torches were really powerful, highlighting the footprints he and Eva had left earlier. He leaned over the banister and shone them all the way down to the ground floor. It was so nice not to be creeping around dark places any more. He was warm and dry, and he had light. He felt on top of the world.

They were on the fourth floor, where Eva was trying to find a toilet that wasn't too disgusting.

Down below in the stairwell, Ben heard a bang and

a scrape. Then voices. There were people moving about on one of the floors below.

Eva came up behind him, zipping up her drysuit. 'What was that?'

'I don't know.' He went down the steps a little way and shone the lights down. 'Hello?'

'Probably someone else getting warm gear,' said Eva. 'Come on, let's go.'

As they started down the stairs, they saw that the swing door to the diving department was propped open with a scuba tank on a black harness. A man in a rubberized drysuit came out carrying another tank and put it down on the tiled floor.

Ben stopped and turned the torches off. Eva bumped into him.

'What?' she said loudly.

'Ssh,' Ben whispered. 'I've seen those guys before. They were looting in Piccadilly just before you found me. They're not nice.'

In the light from the window, he realized that Eva's expression looked angry. 'They saw you like that and they didn't help you?'

Ben watched the man go back in before replying.

'They thought I was drunk. And they were trying to smash their way into a jeweller's.'

Eva stared after the man.

Ben didn't like the look on her face. He took a pinch of her wetsuit to pull her down the stairs.

She followed reluctantly, still brooding about his story. 'You don't leave someone who's got hypothermia.'

'Look,' whispered Ben, 'that's not as bad as the guy who locked me in a cellar that was filling with water. It's just been one of those days. Come on – if we're quick they won't see us.'

Carefully they went down the staircase. Once they were past Eva looked back at the tanks.

'What do they want those for?'

Ben shrugged. 'I guess there's some more jewellery they couldn't get. Maybe they're planning to dive for it.'

Eva spun on her heel and skipped back up the steps. She bent over the tank and twisted a valve. There was a hiss as gas began to escape.

Ben sprinted back up after her. 'What are you doing?' He put his hand on the tap and tried to close it. 'You can't do that. Someone might get hurt.'

'They left you in a state where you could have died. I'm going to make sure they find it difficult to get away with any more booty.' She turned the tap to open again. This time she kept her hand on the valve so he couldn't close it again.

Ben took hold of her by the shoulders and shook her. 'Stop it. What if they're using these to help with a rescue?' Eva put her hand out to grab the banisters and the air tank rolled towards the top step.

Ben tried to grab the harness but he missed, and it rolled easily, bouncing down the tiled steps with a loud metallic clang.

A figure appeared in the doorway, a sledgehammer raised above his head. Ben saw it descending towards him and rolled out of the way, knocking the other air tank over.

As he did so, the regulator snapped off the top, which released the pressure through the tiny hole – and turned the heavy metal air tank into a rocket.

Ben ducked just in time. The tank torpedoed past his ear and carried on through the thick wooden banisters, smashing a hole and hissing loudly. It ploughed into the wall and veered off, splintering wood and shattering glass.

Ben was crouched against the wall, his head cradled in his arms. He opened one eye and looked down.

He couldn't see Eva, but he noticed a deep dent in the wall, as though a car had crashed into it. Plaster and brickwork crumbled down into the stairwell. The other tank sat hissing and spinning in a circle on the half landing below. Eva must have succeeded in loosening the regulator.

Suddenly Ben's head was crushed in a painful grip. 'You little twerp. What do you think you are, some kind of crimefighter?'

Ben twisted his head round and saw the looter reaching for the sledgehammer. He kicked it out of the way and knocked the looter over. The two of them crashed down the stairs – down towards the other tank.

'Ben!' yelled Eva's voice. 'Get away from it!'

Oh, that's brilliant, thought Ben. How exactly do I do that? He caught sight of the man's partner in the doorway, keeping his distance.

The looter had him around the throat. He tried to

pull away but the man's grip was strong. The tank spun in a circle, smashing into his shins and knees. The looter pushed Ben's face closer to the whirling tank. He continued to struggle, wondering if this tank was about to go off like a rocket too? He managed to grab the banister to pull himself away, but it snapped immediately.

He could hear Eva screaming: 'Get off him, get off him!' She was down below him. How had she managed to get down there when he had ended up grappling on the landing?

The looter lost his grip on Ben's collar and grabbed at his head. Ben wrenched himself free, leaving his neoprene cap behind. The whirling cylinder was still spinning round between them. The looter kicked out at it and Ben flattened himself against the wall as it clattered past him.

A sound from below made the whole group freeze. A voice talking over a radio.

'Do you copy?'

'Possible intruder action,' came the reply. 'Proceeding with caution.'

There were footsteps coming up the stairs. Torches

played over the walls and between the banisters.

The looters looked at each other in horror. They forgot about Ben and Eva and scrambled up the stairs again. Something glittery slid out of the man's pocket and caught on the edge of the banisters for a moment, then slithered into the blackness.

The footsteps stopped. There was a scraping noise as something was picked up off the floor. 'Sir, we've got what looks like a very valuable necklace here. There are looters in the store.'

There was a loud crack. It was the kind of noise that not many people hear in real life, but when they do they know exactly what it means. It was followed by a smell of smoke and gunpowder, like a firework going off.

They had just been shot at.

Chapter Thirty-one

Eva hared up the steps towards Ben, who immediately caught her panic. He followed her through a pair of fire doors, barely thinking, taken over by an instinct to run.

Whoever the soldiers caught first they would assume had stolen the necklace. And technically Eva and Ben were looters because they had taken things from the store, even though it was for survival.

They were running for their lives. They pushed past racks of skimpy gym clothes and trainers. At least they gave them some cover. The looters had disappeared.

In front of them they saw a window. It suddenly shattered and they heard a shot from behind.

If they carried on rushing around like this, they would just run into more trouble. Ben needed to think.

He spotted a rack of black rugby gear and rugger-tackled Eva into it. In their black drysuits they blended in, and they watched the soldiers hurrying past, shouting, pushing racks of clothes aside with the muzzles of their guns. The three of them passed close to where Eva and Ben lay huddled, and headed off towards the cash desk and some changing rooms.

Ben waited until they were out of sight, then pulled Eva up. There was a fire exit opposite him. He fell on the door and pushed the bar open.

They ran down the stairs; Ben's brain was racing even faster than his feet. They had to be quick, now that they were out in the open again. Down one flight he saw the entrance for the country clothing section, just as the soldiers entered the top of the stairwell.

Ben grabbed Eva and tore off her hood. He threw it further down the steps, so that the soldiers would think they had just carried straight on down. She stopped and looked at him, her hair springing out in tight corkscrew curls, her eyes wide with the sheer panic of the chase. So that's what it's like to scalp a Teletubby, thought Ben, and dragged her into the country clothing department.

They ran past racks of tweed and Barbours. Ben saw another fire exit and ran for it. Down another flight of stairs and they shouldered open another door, and found themselves out in the street.

Ben had never been so grateful to be back out in the rain again.

They were in Lower Regent Street, which sloped down into the grey water. Just below them, on the tarmac, lay a small dinghy. Ben sprinted towards it, pushed it into the water and pulled Eva in.

He had a moment of déjà vu: it was like his cousins' boat in Macclesfield. The starter cord in the same place, the tiller the same. Ben pulled the starter cord and it started first time. He guided it slowly out into the water.

Then he flopped back and relaxed, exhausted. The chase was over. They'd got away.

For once the rain felt refreshing. Running in the

drysuit, especially with thermals on, was hot work.

'Handy boat,' said Ben. 'I wonder who it belongs to.'

'Hey, look,' said Eva. She pointed back at the shore-line, where Lower Regent Street rose up out of the water.

Two figures in black were standing at the shore, watching Ben and Eva in the boat. The looters.

'Ah,' said Ben. 'Let's hope we don't meet them again. They probably won't be very friendly.'

'I bet they stole it,' said Eva. 'Who knows who it really belongs to?' She shifted a small rucksack out of the way to sit more comfortably.

The three soldiers came out of the fire exit and surrounded the looters, guns held up to their shoulders, ready to fire. Those few moments watching Ben in their stolen boat had cost the looters dearly.

For a horrible moment Ben thought they were going to be shot there and then. But then, reluctantly, they put their hands up.

Eva shook out her hair and settled back. 'Serves them right,' she commented. Her restful pose didn't last long. Suddenly she wrinkled her nose and sat up. 'It smells filthy out here.'

Now that she mentioned it, Ben had to agree. It reminded him of a camping trip he'd taken with his cousins last August. The tent with the chemical toilet had got so smelly they decided they'd rather go in the bushes.

'Where are we going?' said Eva.

For a moment Ben's mind was a blank. He knew he'd been going somewhere, but the excitement had driven it out of his mind. Then he saw a road sign. Buckingham Palace to the right, Charing Cross to the left. Of course.

'Charing Cross,' he said. 'Someone should be waiting for me there. I hope . . .'

Francisco heard movement outside the station. Something stirring the water very slowly, like a boat.

He looked through the arches and saw a figure in a dark jacket moving outside. He seemed to be sitting astride a big motorbike and moving it very slowly through the water, seesawing from side to side as though he was pushing it with his feet.

He squinted at the hat the man was wearing. White and red checks. A City policeman.

Quite an enterprising policeman. He was using the heavy motorbike as an anchor to enable him to make his way across the current.

Francisco thought quickly. Had José remained in captivity? Had he had to confess about their rendezvous location?

Why was a policeman coming in here now?

Francisco checked the clip of the Beretta and clicked the safety catch off with his thumb. He stayed where he was, sitting in the locker. It was good cover. Besides, if he moved, the policeman would hear the splash.

He glanced at the white puff in the water: the body of the tramp lay face down, nosing against a news stand. If the policeman saw that, his suspicions might be aroused. Francisco was ready to drop him.

The policeman reached the arch and dropped the motorcycle. It crashed against the wall and subsided into the water.

Interesting, thought Francisco. He didn't think policemen were generally that careless with property.

The figure stood at the archway and looked around, then stared over at the left luggage lockers.

Francisco stiffened.

The policeman waded forwards and took his hat off.

Francisco put his gun down and called out in Spanish. 'José, you idiot. I nearly shot you.'

José grinned. 'Better late than never.' He splashed over to Francisco and they embraced.

Francisco examined José's costume. 'Good outfit. It fooled me.' Only now did he notice that José didn't have the right trousers to go with the police jacket, but they had been almost covered by the water.

José shrugged. 'It's been useful.' He opened their locker and looked in.

Francisco patted his pockets. 'I've got the maps and some basics.' He handed José a Swiss Army knife.

José put it in his pocket. 'Have you got your cuffs off?'

Francisco showed him his wrists, still bloodied under the cuffs. 'Made a bit of a mess. Wish we'd packed some antibiotics. What did you do with yours?'

José held up his wrists. His cuffs were still there too. 'Boltcutters.' He rummaged in the locker. 'Did you take all the money? You could at least give me some.'

'I didn't know if you were going to show.'

José put his hand out. 'Half each. In case we get separated. That's what we agreed.'

Francisco reached into his pocket and took out the folded wad of notes. He split it and gave half to José, along with one of the fake passports. José tucked the money into the pocket of his dark jeans.

'Have you got our route sorted?'

Francisco nodded. 'Now we just need a boat.'

Ben piloted the dinghy into Trafalgar Square. Ahead was Nelson's Column, just on the edge of the water-line. Passing in front of it in a small boat was a group of people in scarlet coats and gold buttons. They wore strange hats, rather like the three-cornered hat Nelson was wearing. It looked like a uniform of some kind, but it wasn't one that Ben had seen before. Their boat, which they were rowing in a slow but dogged fashion, looked as though it had come out of a museum. It was heavily varnished like a piece of antique furniture. But it was a day for strange sights.

'You're kidding,' Eva was saying. 'Your mother isn't really Bel Kelland? She came to give a speech at my college debating society in my final year. My boyfriend had to show her around – he was terrified of her.'

'Yeah, my dad doesn't like her much either.'

Eva pointed over to a building like a dirty grey wedding cake. A series of arches ran along the bottom. 'Charing Cross is just up there. I can't wait to meet her.' She actually looked quite excited at the prospect.

Ben felt a bit sick. If Bel wasn't there, what would he do then? He hadn't given it any thought. He'd spent all that time just trying to get here. Now that Charing Cross was actually in sight, he had to face up to the possibility.

He took the boat up to one of the arches in front of the entrance. It was too narrow to fit through. He craned his neck round, but couldn't see inside the station. He turned back to Eva. 'You stay here. If I wedge the boat in, it shouldn't go anywhere. I just need to see if she's there.'

Eva looked at the deserted concourse, eager for a glimpse of the famous Dr Kelland. 'I don't see anyone, apart from those two guys over by the left luggage.'

One of the two figures started to wade in their direction and they saw that he was a policeman, the band around his hat red and white instead of the usual black and white.

'I didn't think the police had hats like that,' said Ben.

'The City of London police do,' said Eva.

Ben waved to him. The policeman spotted him and began to wade purposefully towards them. The guy with him still had his back to them; he was carrying a rucksack and wore a jacket with a big logo on the back.

The policeman looked very wet, as though he'd had a hell of a day too. There were smears of mud on his black raincoat. The other guy looked dry. Ben assumed the policeman must be one of the evacuation party.

'Hi,' said Ben. 'I know this sounds silly, but I'd arranged to meet my mum here . . .'

'Can you pilot this boat?' said the policeman. He had a strange accent; strongly Spanish.

That was unusual, Ben thought. Then he looked more closely at the other man. Why did he look familiar?

'Yes,' he replied.

The policeman grabbed the ropes on the side of the dinghy and climbed in. The other man turned, handed his rucksack to the policeman and began to wade over. Now Ben could see his face.

Suddenly everything seemed to slow down. The guy's face. The bloodied marks on his wrists. He knew him!

Eva made a strangled noise, like she'd had a shock.

Then Ben saw the gun in the policeman's hand, pressed against Eva's temple.

Chapter Thirty-two

The sub captain looked at the chronometer, its figures starkly green in the red background light of the conn. Still, there had been no contact from Whitehall.

The helmsman watched the depth gauge display, then turned around. 'Captain, we're ascending to the surface now.'

Once again, the sub was risking discovery by coming to the surface to send a signal.

'Communications Officer, prepare to deploy the radio mast.'

'Radio mast is ready to deploy, sir.'

'Sir.' The navigation officer turned round. 'We've got something in the water above us.'

The captain was at his side immediately, looking at the sonar screen. The sweeping orange arm was high-lighting a spot just north-west of them. It was travelling slowly – in their direction.

The navigation officer checked his other instruments. 'By the way it's moving it's been dropped into the water from a plane, sir.'

The captain straightened up. This could be enemy action. Or it could be something else . . . 'Helmsman, abandon current manoeuvre. Hold your position. Weapons officer, check out the object.'

His next order was pre-empted. The communi-cations officer spoke. 'Sir, it's attempting to make contact. It's a sonar signal.'

The entire conn held its breath. The captain spoke. 'What nationality is it?'

The communications officer double-checked his instruments before answering. 'British, sir. Whitehall's back on line. They must have sent a Nimrod to drop a radio buoy.'

They couldn't relax yet. What was the message?

Would they get the all-clear? Or were they going to continue to follow sealed orders and possibly fire on an enemy country?

On the communications officer's console, a red light came on. Beside it, a tongue of white paper like a till roll slowly curled out of a printer.

'Captain,' said the communications officer. He tore the sheet of paper free.

The captain went and took the sheet of paper, scan-reading it.

When he looked up, it was as though a black shadow had lifted from his face. 'Gentlemen, we are to stand down. I'm going to talk to the crew.'

In the skies above the Atlantic, a Nimrod jet flew in a wide circle, leaving a vapour trail over the water like a halo. It was a state-of-the-art aircraft, carrying the latest communications equipment. It had just dropped a sonar signal into the water near the submarine. And now it was waiting for a very important message.

The communications officer looked up from his console and gave a thumbs up.

That was it. The sub had acknowledged the

message. The signal had been dropped in the right spot. Down in the deep steel-grey water, the sub was returning to normal duties.

The Nimrod's job was done. It completed its last circle and headed straight for home.

Francisco crouched down low in the boat next to Eva. He had a knife, which he kept pressed against her leg, his fist curled round the knuckleduster handle, its brass curls showing between his fingers. That alone looked brutal enough. With his other hand he kept his jacket hood up over his head. José got down next to Ben. He kept the gun against Ben's knee; with his other hand he pointed up the river. 'Drive.'

Ben did exactly as he was asked. The gun and the knife were like some kind of over-ride switch in his head. The black muzzle and that vicious blade were all he could see.

He took the boat across the bottom end of Trafalgar Square, then down towards the Embankment. Once he reached the course of the river proper, he opened the throttle.

He misjudged. This wasn't anything like zipping

across the empty reservoirs in the Peak District and Macclesfield Forest. The river was full of obstacles: bridges, vehicles, other boats. Not only that, the current was at its most fierce here. In moments it whipped him around through 180 degrees, and the solid bulk of Hungerford railway bridge was racing towards him, like a giant iron girder with a train parked on top. He pulled the tiller hard left and an enormous wash of stinking water rained down into the boat. With one eye open he narrowly avoided a drifting bus and looped a circle around the London Eye and the ArBonCo Centre.

José dug the pistol into his leg. 'West,' he said roughly.

On the third circle Ben had managed to slow down the boat a little. The soft hull scraped against the top of a lamppost. He looked down, trying to thread between them, but he was still going too fast and he scraped the entire row of them.

It didn't help his concentration having the gun pointed at him: he kept finding his gaze wandering back to it.

An army dinghy chugged by, full of rescued people

huddling under tarpaulins to keep dry. It was going at half the speed Ben was. The soldier at the tiller shouted at him, the words lost in the whine of the engine. He obviously wasn't impressed by Ben's driving. Ben looked back at him helplessly. Maybe he would see they were at gunpoint. But José and Francisco kept down low. They must be worried they might be recognized. Ben tried sending desperate thoughts towards the soldiers. *Look at us*, he telepathed. *Can't you see they've got a gun?*

The wind flung rain into his face, and by the time Ben opened his eyes again the soldiers were long gone and he was trying to focus on what he would hit next. As well as checking out the gun sticking in his knee. And the knife.

His eyes sent his brain a snapshot of Eva, huddled down next to Francisco, staring at his blade.

A Chinook was hanging over a bridge in the distance, figures dangling from its winch like toys on a mobile. Ben was so busy looking at it that he almost didn't see that Westminster Bridge was straight in front of him. Another sharp turn and he was whizzing over the terrace in front of the Houses of Parliament, his reflection speeding past its gothic windows. He circled around the entire building, passing between the railings at the front and Westminster Abbey. The *Cutty Sark* rocked in his wake. He swept around to the front and into the main drag of the river again. Circling seemed the only way to slow down. Still, he'd got past the bridge.

He hoped there weren't any news cameras in any of those helicopters. If his dad or his cousins ever saw this, he'd never be allowed in a boat again. That's if he and Eva got out of this alive. Probably the only reason they were alive at the moment was that there were so many people around. Otherwise Francisco and José would have disposed of them straight away.

What would happen once they got into a less busy part of the river?

Just behind him a Chinook stopped over Westminster Bridge and let its winch down. Ben swung the boat round in a big circle, making an S shape. He nearly rammed a boat coming the other way, full of more of those men in the scarlet uniforms with the multicoloured medal ribbons. Ben did a tight circle around them, spelling out an O, then started another S.

SOS. For the benefit of the audience in the sky.

José seemed to have had enough of Ben's erratic sea-manship. He dragged him away from the controls and took the tiller himself. Ben had got his message out just in time. That is, if the Chinook above had seen.

The bottom of the boat humped as it rasped over a submerged object. Ben saw a concrete shelter like a bus stop, the water swirling backwards and forwards over it. José looked down, surprised.

Not so easy to steer this thing, is it? gloated Ben.

The next bridge was going to be tricky. A big old brown building with tall Tudor windows stood close to it, forming a bottleneck for the water-borne traffic. It was like a blind corner on a bend.

Suddenly a small motorboat was coming towards them from the other direction. Ben caught a glimpse of two figures in Barbour jackets, waving at José. There was no way that both craft could get through that narrow gap at the same time.

José slid the rudder hard left, and the dinghy was buffeted against the motorboat, side on. Fibreglass hull scraped against the rubber of the dinghy. José stood up and cocked the Beretta. 'Out of the way.'

In the boat were a couple in their fifties, their possessions lying in plastic boxes around their feet. They looked at José and the gun with wide, fearful eyes.

The woman put her hands up. She was trying to talk but the words wouldn't come. The man grabbed something from the dashboard and raised it. It was a stubby-looking gun: a flare pistol.

'Don't shoot,' he called, but his hand was shaking. 'We're just trying to get away from town.' The boat bobbed up and down on the choppy water, making the gun wave crazily, as if he was trying to draw something in the air with the muzzle.

'We'll go back,' said his wife. She grabbed the wheel and tried to manoeuvre the boat out of the way.

Her husband wasn't expecting that. He lost his balance and a bright flash of orange light shot towards the dinghy like a torpedo.

Ben huddled next to Eva on the floor of the dinghy. The flare hit the water less than a metre away from them and exploded in a plume of brown water.

When Ben raised his head, his hair was full of filthy

water. Eva was cowering next to Francisco, who was shaking water out of his eyes, feeling for his knife on the floor of the dinghy with the other hand.

Ben saw it all in slow motion. The man in the other boat was looking terrified. Firing the flare pistol was obviously an accident, but José was rising to his knees, the Beretta ready to fire back.

Ben hunched into a ball and rolled into him. José fell forwards and pulled the trigger at the same moment, and the bullet bored straight through the side of the dinghy. There was a massive explosion.

Then they were in the water, the dinghy reduced to scraps of burning rubber. Ben could see Eva swirling away in the current, her mouth gasping and screaming, as if she was no more than a disembodied head. He saw the white hull of the motorboat coming up and tried to grab at it, but before he could get his arm out of the water, he had slid past it.

He went under and came back up again. Something hidden under the surface banged into his legs, as if he was in the jaws of some flying monster that was dragging him along the ground. A wall hit him in the ribs, so hard that he doubled over with the impact, and his vision was blanked out by river water as he went under again.

When he resurfaced, spitting and gasping, looking for help, all he could see was moving boats, shouting faces. José swirled near to him, like an out-of-control dodgem. He was hunched over the stalled engine, trying to use it to stay afloat. The remains of the flare still fizzed in the water and burning scraps of dinghy sent wisps of smoke up into the rainy air.

Ben went under again. As he kicked to the surface, his feet met something solid; a bridge parapet perhaps. His feet struggled to get a purchase on something. Then suddenly he caught sight of a big shape moving past in the water: a pale grey triangular fin like a sail; an empty-looking black eye. A circuit completed in his brain and he waited to see the words: SEE THE TIGER SHARK AT THE LONDON AQUARIUM. How come that cardboard notice was still here?

A wave washed over him so he didn't see that there were no words. Just a long expanse of grey solid flesh. Flesh that was moving, rippling as the tail swished from side to side.

Ben's feet found his perch and his eyes opened

again. The next thing he saw was Francisco being swept past, the water catching at his rucksack and pulling him along. Ben saw the terrorist's arms and legs paddling wildly as he rose and fell in the water.

The cut-out shark came past again. It felt like something big was slicing through the water; something as big as a boat. Then Ben glimpsed a flap-like mouth and a big set of open jaws lined with ragged teeth.

That wasn't a cardboard shark. It was real.

Ben knew that sharks were attracted by the frantic scrabbling of a struggling swimmer, but his instincts to escape drove all sensible thought out of his mind. His feet started running along the invisible wall beneath him, his arms splashing about wildly. He launched himself backwards – anything to get away from that killing machine.

As he sank down into the water again, he tried to kick up, but his feet hit empty water. Without his foothold he couldn't stay afloat . . . couldn't breathe. He struck out with his arms.

Then something grabbed him. Was it the shark?

Chapter Thirty-three

They say a drowning man comes up three times. Ben came up and saw Eva's face. With one hand she was grasping the neck of his suit; with the other it seemed like she was trying to hit him. Ben went under and was dragged up again, spitting and gasping as his mouth filled with foul water. Eva tried to punch him again. This time she got him – hard in the middle of the chest.

There was a loud hissing noise, and then she stopped trying to hit him.

Ben realized he was floating: he wasn't having to keep himself above the water. The suit felt tighter around his shoulders and chest.

Eva was bobbing beside him, her arms out in a T-shape beside her. 'You can stop struggling. I just hit your buoyancy valve.'

Where was the shark? Ben spluttered out a warning. It didn't come out as words, only water.

A few metres away they heard a piercing scream and Ben saw Francisco's flailing arms and the nose of the tiger shark like the cone of a rocket. Its jaw dropped open and closed around Francisco's middle.

The sound was cut off as abruptly as it had started.

Ben and Eva stayed bobbing in the water, stunned. They seemed to have been swept out of the fierce Thames current. It was no longer a struggle to stay in one place. The top of a tree was sticking up out of the water just a few metres away, and beyond that was the hurly-burly of travelling boats and flood detritus.

They were in some kind of enclosure, like a walled garden. It must belong to the big Tudor building.

And hopefully the shark was still out there with all the rest of the traffic.

Eva was the first to speak. 'He was bleeding. That's why the shark was attracted to him.'

Ben remembered the wounds on Francisco's wrists. Then he had another thought. 'Eva, don't you think it's weird that there's a shark in the Thames?'

She made a movement, like a shrug, her hands waving gently in the water. 'There have been porpoises and whales in the Thames before. A shark is par for the course.'

Ben couldn't fathom her. She reminded him of a very serious teacher at his school, who never laughed or looked surprised at anything.

Eva certainly was a strange girl. But now she had saved his life twice.

Eva swam towards the building and Ben followed. They climbed in through a window like two floundering fish, leaving splashes on the polished oak floor.

Outside, in the water, José couldn't see Francisco. He was clinging desperately to a lamppost, but the current was battering against him, trying to shake him loose. His police hat had gone and no one could see the markings on the jacket.

The current was winning.

Then José saw a boat coming towards him and made a desperate bid to swim to it. With a superhuman effort he reached its varnished sides and thankfully slapped a hand onto it.

Something hard and wooden came down on his hands. As he fell back into the water he saw an old guy in a black hat like Nelson's and a red coat with gold buttons, holding a cricket bat.

José submerged and came back up. His ears were full of water but he could see the man's lips moving.

'Oh no you don't.'

Clive Brooks, Sidney Cadogan, Madeleine Harwood and Fat Pinstripe were sitting around a large dining table in one of the bunker's wood-panelled private dining rooms. The furniture was mahogany. There were even heavy brocade curtains to give the impression of a normal room with windows.

Despite the opulence, Fat Pinstripe was worrying about the accommodation. 'If we have to stay down here for months, we need to get organized. We should form a bunker committee. Get some rules in this place. Some of these facilities and supplies should be restricted access.'

'No we don't,' said Bel tartly. 'Instead of counting

the toilet rolls, we need to worry about why we ended up here in the first place and work out how to stop it happening again.'

'You can stay here,' said a voice at the door, 'or you can come with us and leave by the Camden entrance. Once you've signed the Official Secrets Act, of course, to cover this incident.'

Standing outside in the corridor were two soldiers in disruption-pattern uniform and neat berets.

Bel didn't hang around. She was the first out into the corridor. More soldiers were going through the rooms and preparing the evacuation. The corridor was teeming with people, like an airport departure lounge. They seemed to be heading in the general direction of one corridor, filing past a soldier with a palm pilot.

Bel went up to the soldier. 'Have you evacuated the ArBonCo Centre or Charing Cross yet?'

'We're getting around to all those places in good time, ma'am. Are you looking for someone in particular?'

'My son. I was meant to be meeting him.'

The soldier touched the stylus on his screen a couple

of times, then handed the palm pilot to Bel. 'Right, ma'am. Put your details in and the details of any people you're looking for. Then, when we pick your son up, the database will flag that we've got you too.'

Bel thought it sounded dubious: what were the chances that another Ben Tracey was wandering the capital today? But the form asked for plenty of details: her home address, date of birth, middle names; and the same for Ben. She filled it in, handed the palm pilot back and peered at the screen over the soldier's shoulder.

'So, have you got him?'

'We can't tell you that yet, ma'am, we have to hook up to the satellite. But as soon as we get back to the rescue centre we do a match for all the people we've picked up. We've matched a lot of people already.'

She stepped away and joined the stream of people starting the walk towards the Camden entrance. How long would she have to wait?

Ahead of her, a tall figure in a suit was getting directions from a soldier with a clipboard. He had sandy-coloured hair and a shirt with an open collar that revealed a healthy outdoor tan. Bel's sharp eyes recognized him immediately from news pictures: David Atkinson, the Prime Minister of Canada. He had been down here all the time, in another part of the bunker.

She set off dodging through the crowd like a rugger player going for a try, crumpled purple sleeves pushed up purposefully.

Chapter Thirty-four

Ben and Eva heard the pounding of the helicopter out-side but they'd stopped getting excited at the sound. So many had gone overhead already and hadn't stopped for them. And anyway, it wasn't as if they were a rescue priority. They were safe enough inside the building. And at least in their drysuits they were warm.

Whatever the building was, it was very old, and the room they were in was interesting to explore. The windows were stained glass, the curtains heavy velvet with gold embroidery. Gold candlesticks stood on a big stone mantelpiece. A big gilded mirror reflected the dull rainy sky outside.

Ben had hung one of the big, gold-embroidered curtains out of the window to attract rescuers' attention. In the meantime, Eva was looking at some old books on the shelves while Ben was trying to get the zip undone on his drysuit. It was doing too good a job of keeping him warm now. He peered in the mirror, trying to get hold of the tag to ease it open.

He got the shock of his life when he saw, behind his reflection, the figure dangling on a rope in the window.

He whirled round. The helicopter outside must have stopped for them. A man was hanging there in an abseil harness, beckoning them to come outside.

Eva and Ben reached the window at the same time.

Their rescuer was a soldier in khaki fatigues and a khaki-painted helmet. He held out another sling.

Ben gestured to Eva to go first, and she stepped onto the window ledge. The soldier gave her the sling while he signalled to Ben to turn round so that he could grasp him around the middle with his legs; then he gave a thumbs-up signal to the winch operator waiting above.

As the winch pulled them up, Ben took a last look

down at the dirty river water, the surface corrugated by the helicopter's downdraught. The noise of the heli became louder and louder, and by the time they had been winched up into its belly, it was deafening.

The winchman waved Ben and Eva towards some seats at the front, where several people were already sitting huddled in foil survival blankets. Ben headed for an empty seat and the heli lurched, nearly depositing him in the lap of a pretty woman in a green helmet and a dark blue jumpsuit. He regained his balance and sat down heavily opposite her instead.

Eva was already sitting down. She nudged Ben and pointed at the logo on the pretty woman's jumpsuit. It said CAPITAL RADIO FLYING EYE. Below that was embroidered a name: MEENA CHOHAN.

Meena caught Eva's eye and gave them both a friendly smile. Eva leaned forward eagerly, trying to talk to her, but the noise through the open door reduced their conversation to sign language. Still, Ben found it amusing to see Eva impressed by something at last.

Meena handed Ben a Palm Pilot with a stylus. It was a register for the rescue authorities. He added his details and scrolled back through the previous entries. Judging by the number of names and addresses already there, the heli had picked up a lot of people during the course of the day. One of them had the same name as the Prime Minister. Ben pointed to it as he handed the Palm Pilot over to Eva. He was sceptical that it was really the Prime Minister, though; the joker had even given the home address as Downing Street.

Eva shrugged. So politicians didn't faze her; she seemed a lot more impressed with Meena.

Ben, on the other hand, was impressed with the controls of the heli. The pilot, who had the name Dorek painted in white lettering on the back of his helmet, was bringing it down to a hover again. Ben was fascinated by his constant, gentle adjustments with the central stick, as though the heli was a living thing. Suddenly he realized how much he would like, himself, to learn to fly one day.

Behind the seats, the winch crew were set to go out again. The soldier standing by the winch checked the cable, then gave a thumbs-up. His partner gave a last check to his abseil harness and jumped smartly out of the door.

Ben looked out of the tiny window by his seat. The winch crew were targeting a roof terrace littered with hospital trolleys, beside an L-shaped building. A handful of people were sitting on the trolleys huddled under blankets, as though they were the last stragglers of a much bigger evacuation.

It was just a stone's throw from the ArBonCo Centre. How funny, thought Ben. I can't seem to keep away from the place.

Meena was tapping him on the shoulder. He turned round and she passed him the Palm Pilot again. Ben saw that, on the screen, his name was flashing: someone was looking for him. A Dr Bel Kelland, now at the Camden centre.

Ben stayed looking at the name for a few minutes, a smile on his face. His mum was safe.

More survivors were reeled in. The winchman made sure they were well inside the cabin and away from the door before taking the harness off. When they had all been picked up, his partner slid the doors shut and gave the pilot the signal that they were secure. As Dorek took the heli higher and away downriver, Ben took a last look down at the ArBonCo building, surrounded by water. Smoke curled gently out of the lower floors but the upper floors looked intact. Perhaps he could have stayed in there the whole time after all. There were many times that day when he'd wished he had.

He still had the Palm Pilot in his hands. He looked at the message next to his name and smiled wryly. Camden. He needn't have bothered trying to get to Charing Cross after all.

An evacuee with black spiky hair sat down in the seat beside him. He passed her the Palm Pilot and watched as she entered her name.

He had seen that name before. That morning, a lifetime ago, on the label of a suitcase. Ben looked at her face properly.

'Vicky?' he said. 'Vicky James?'

With the door closed, the heli was quieter and it was possible to talk. 'I'm Ben. We met at Waterloo this morning.'

Vicky's face lit up as recognition dawned. She flung her arms around Ben and hugged him tight. She smelled of antiseptic, of hospitals and dirty water.

Eva looked on, bemused.

Vicky passed the Palm Pilot to another evacuee and sat back. She ran a hand through her hair, making it stick up even more, and let out a long sigh. 'Boy, am I glad today's over.'

Her mood was catching. Meena and Ben nodded slowly.

Even Eva looked relieved – a little. She said ruefully: 'I only came down to do a bit of shopping for my diving holiday.'

In moments the other three were roaring with laughter.

Meena was the first to recover. 'Looks like your holiday started early.' She wiped a tear from her eye.

Vicky looked at Ben for a moment, then launched herself at him for another hug. 'I can't believe it's you.'

With his face muffled in the two fleeces she was wearing, Ben struggled to breathe. But he hugged her back. It was so good to see her. Perhaps it was because he'd seen so many other people who hadn't been so lucky. On the Embankment, in the ArBonCo offices, in the London Eye, in the river, in the streets, in the Tube station. His odyssey to get here must have taken him past hundreds of people who had been in the wrong place at the wrong time, randomly taken by the water. Now, finally, one of the faces in the crowd had beaten the odds.

'Sorry,' said Vicky, sitting back and composing herself. 'I'm probably embarrassing you.' She put her hand out for a high-five. 'Hey, we made it.'

First Meena high-fived her; then, quietly, Eva. Finally Ben met her proffered hand enthusiastically. 'Yeah,' he grinned. 'We made it.'

ALPHA FORCE

If you enjoyed this book, you'll also enjoy the *Alpha Force* series by Chris Ryan. Turn over to read an extract from the first title in the series, *Survival . . .*

SOMEWHERE IN THE INDONESIAN ARCHIPELAGO

It only takes an instant to die . . .

As he struggled to swim away from the huge wave that towered over him, Alex began to hear his father's voice in his head, patiently explaining the survival skills he had learned in the SAS. It was oddly comforting to listen to that calm, quiet voice and Alex found the strength to push himself on through the turbulent water, even though his muscles were almost useless with exhaustion.

It only takes an instant to die, continued his father's voice. *The way to survive is to make sure you never reach that instant. Are you listening, Alex? You need to understand how an accident happens. Most people think it explodes without warning - blam! Like a firework. But you look more closely at that accident and what do you see . . .?*

'A fuse . . .' croaked Alex, forcing himself to take a few more strokes before floundering to a stop. 'There's always a fuse . . .'

He blinked the stinging seawater from his eyes and looked over his shoulder to see whether he was clear of the breaking wave. He groaned. All that effort and he had hardly moved. It was as though he had been treading water. The wave still towered over him, even higher now. It was a solid slab of black water, except at the top where there was a frayed edge of white foam. The wave had reached its crest and was beginning to curl over. In a few seconds, the whole weight of that wall of water would crash down on top of him.

Alex stopped swimming. He knew he was fighting a losing battle. Instead, he concentrated on breathing, topping up his system with as much oxygen as he could before the wave hit. He felt himself being tugged backwards as the surrounding water was sucked into the base of the breaking wave. Forcing his burning lungs to take in one more deep breath, he turned and dived down under the surface for a second before the breaker crashed down on top of him.

Even under the water, Alex was overwhelmed by the impact. The breaker slammed him down and knocked all the air out of him with a casual efficiency that reminded him of his mother kneading dough. As he tumbled lazily through the water, drifting on the edge of consciousness, Alex thought about his mother making bread half a world away in the kitchen he had been so keen to leave. He thought of how sad she would be if he did not return from this trip and suddenly he was fully awake again.

He began to struggle against the current, which was still rolling him over and over, pulling him nearer and nearer to the reef where the boat had broken in two. If he was dragged across the razor-sharp coral, his skin would be torn to ribbons. How close was he? There was a roaring in his ears which could be breaking surf. Alex forced his eyes open, but it was so dark under the water, he could not tell which way was up. He redoubled his efforts to swim against the current until he felt as though his chest was about to burst open. His movements became weaker, the roaring in his ears grew louder and sparks of multi-coloured light began to dance behind his eyes, but he kept going and, suddenly, the current let him go. He broke the surface and pulled whooping breaths of air into his lungs.

Clearing his eyes, he peered about him. The moon was up and, in its pale light, he could just see the dark, jagged outline of the island he was trying to reach. He turned in the water and saw white surf breaking on the reef behind him. It was still too close for comfort and another huge wave was beginning to build. Gritting his teeth, Alex started to swim again, scanning the water for any sign of the rest of A-Watch.

He spotted Amber first, way ahead of him. She had nearly reached the island and was swimming strongly. Behind Amber, but still in the quieter waters of the lagoon, two more heads bobbed close together in the water. Paulo and Li, thought Alex, guessing that Paulo would not leave Li's side if he could help it. But where was Hex? Alex felt a chill run through him as he remembered that Hex, the fifth member of A-Watch, had been even nearer to the reef before the wave hit.

Despite the next breaker building behind him, Alex slowed and turned to scan the surface for Hex. He half-expected to see a body, floating face down in a spreading circle of blood, but there was nothing. Then he caught a movement over to his left. There was Hex, ahead of him now, and swimming steadily towards the island. He must have managed to surf in on the back of the wave that had swallowed Alex.

Satisfied, Alex put the others out of his mind and concentrated on swimming as hard as he could. This time he was nearly clear of the breaker when it crashed. Once more, he dived to survive the impact, then swam against the current that was pulling him backwards. He felt a surge of elation as he broke surface again. He was going to make it! Then something slammed into the back of his head with bone-shattering force. Instinctively, he flung his left arm up to protect his head and was caught in a grip which instantly tightened, biting into the flesh of his wrist. As he began to spiral down into the water, trailing blood, Alex heard his father's voice again.

Every accident has a fuse, son. There's always a fuse.

Alex watched with a sort of dazed curiosity as a thin rope of his own blood twisted away from him towards the surface. That must be the fuse, he thought. In the few seconds left to him before he lost consciousness, Alex imagined the fuse stretching across the sea and back in time to twenty-four hours earlier, when they had all still been aboard the *Phoenix*. That was when it had all started. That final Watch Duty, when the fuse was lit . . .

CHAPTER ONE

Alex knelt on the fore-deck of the *Phoenix* as she cut a graceful path through the clear, blue water. The *Phoenix* was a beautiful ship; a newly-built replica of a three-mastered schooner with white sails that curved like wings in the breeze. She was a week into her maiden voyage, sailing east across the Java Sea. To the south, the island of Java made a jagged scribble on the horizon and all around them clusters of smaller Indonesian islands dotted the water. The late-afternoon sun touched everything with a soft, golden glow.

Alex had no time to gaze at the view. He was concentrating on polishing the brass fittings of the deck rail to a high shine. His back ached and his chest and arms were beaded with sweat in the humid heat of the day, but, for the first time since the voyage began, he was happy. A-Watch were nearly at the end of their latest Watch Duty and, for once, nothing had gone wrong. Heather, their Watch leader, had been determined to have a good Watch. She had set them their tasks and then spent the whole four hours circling the deck, watching them coldly like a small, blue-eyed shark.

Alex glanced at the other four members of A-Watch. Amber and Hex were both hunched over a big, metal cookpot, preparing vegetables. They were working in a sullen silence and trading hostile looks, but at least they weren't fighting. Li was up in the rigging, clambering and balancing high above the deck with the confidence of an expert climber. Alex was not sure how much work Li was doing up there, but he supposed anything was better than the total lack of interest she had shown so far. Paulo was swabbing the deck. He had started off well, but now he was absent-mindedly pushing his mop back and forth over one very clean patch of deck while he gazed up at Li, hypnotized by her slim legs and the swing of her silky black hair.

'Paulo!'

Paulo jumped. Heather was standing with her hands on her hips, glaring at him. He swallowed, then tried one of his trademark heart-melting smiles. The smile turned to a look of horror as Heather stalked across the deck towards him, her eyes like chips of ice. Grabbing the mop, Paulo moved off, swabbing at high speed and sending water flying everywhere. Alex grinned as he turned back to his polishing. Heather was tiny but very scary. She was in her mid-twenties, he guessed, which made her barely ten years older than the five members of her Watch, but she had started work aboard sail-training ships like the *Phoenix* at sixteen and she was as hard as nails.

Alex gave the brasswork one last swipe and straightened up, rubbing his aching back. He caught the tiniest nod of approval from Heather and grinned again. This trip might just start working out after all.

'Not bad,' said Heather, looking around the deck. 'Not *good*,' she scowled, folding her arms. 'But – it's a start. Now, listen up. B-Watch'll be relieving us here any minute, so let's get this deck ship-shape for them. Paulo and

Alex, stow away your cleaning stuff. Hex and Amber, carry that cookpot down to the galley. Together! Li, enough of the circus act. Come down and take a bow. I'm off to write up the Watch log.'

Heather walked away and Alex breathed a sigh of relief. The Watch was over and nothing had gone wrong. He was beginning to think there might be some hope for A-Watch. He was mistaken.

As soon as Heather was out of sight, Hex dropped his side of the cookpot.

'Hey!' yelled Amber, jumping out of the way as water slopped onto the deck.

Hex ignored her. Pulling his palmtop from the pouch at his belt, he flipped it open and sat down with his back against the mast. His fingers keyed the air and he stared at the screen with a hungry look on his face as he waited for the machine to wake up.

Amber's dark eyes flashed as she glared down at Hex. 'Look at you,' she spat. 'Junkie hacker. Can't you cope with real life?'

'Not when you're in it,' muttered Hex.

Li hooted with laughter as she climbed down the last stretch of rope webbing. 'Way to go, Hex. Straight through the heart. You win the Mr Nasty prize for today.' She paused for an instant, looking down to check out her next foothold, and Paulo threw down his mop.

'Do not worry, Li,' he said, leaping to the base of the mast. 'I am here.'

Paulo reached out his hands to her and Li looked at him with raised eyebrows, then threw herself backwards off the rigging. Flipping over in mid-air, she landed neatly with her arms outstretched and her uplifted eyes full of mischief. The thud of her feet hitting the deck startled Hex, making him look away from his screen for an instant. It was enough for Amber. She swooped down and snatched the palmtop, sprinting away with it as Hex struggled to his feet.

'You are dead!' yelled Hex and Amber laughed over her shoulder at him.

That was when the accident exploded across

the deck. Still looking behind her, Amber ran full pelt into Paulo's discarded mop. The wooden handle smacked into her shins, knocking her off her feet and sending her hurtling across the deck. The palmtop flew through the air and disappeared over the side. In an instant that seemed to last for ever, Alex saw that Amber was either going to follow the palmtop into the sea, or smash her skull against the deck rail.

Without stopping to think, Alex put his head down and launched himself at Amber in an attempt to knock her off-course. The impact jarred every bone in his body and stopped his breath. For one, stunned second, he felt as though he was floating in mid-air, then he landed hard on the deck, knocking the remaining breath from his lungs and grating the skin from his elbow.

Alex sucked in air and blinked rapidly to clear his vision. Had he succeeded? He did not dare to look behind him. Instead, he looked up at Li, Hex and Paulo. All three of them were wearing identical shocked expressions. Alex closed his eyes, imagining the worst. Then a fist thumped him squarely in the back.

'You prize moron!'

Dizzily, Alex got to his knees and turned round. A relieved grin spread across his face. Amber was standing over him and she looked furious.

'You think that was funny?' yelled Amber. 'See what you did?' She thrust a grazed and bleeding knee in front of his nose. The wound looked startlingly pink against her black skin.

Alex stopped grinning. 'Sorry,' he muttered. 'I was just—'

'He was just saving your miserable life,' interrupted Hex, with an icy edge to his voice.

'Oh, puh-leeze,' sneered Amber.

'It's true,' said Li. 'Alex stopped you from going overboard.'

'Yeah, right,' said Amber uncertainly, peering over the deck rail.

'Really, he did,' said Paulo. 'You were about to follow that palmtop into the sea.'

Amber looked at Paulo, then at Hex. 'Your palmtop? In the sea . . .?'

Hex nodded grimly. Amber looked down at her feet. When she raised her head again, there was a smile of pure delight on her face.

'Your precious palmtop . . .?' She mimed a clownish dive and snorted with laughter.

Hex snapped. He started towards Amber, his green eyes flat and merciless. Amber grinned and settled into a fighting stance, her feet apart for balance. Hex was broad-shouldered and muscled, but Amber matched him in height and her reflexes had been sharpened by training in the sports only rich girls get to play. Years of fencing, archery and downhill skiing had taught her all about balance, avoidance, concentration and speed. Amber felt more than ready to meet Hex head-on but, before the fight could start, a wave of cold water knocked them both sideways. They stopped in their tracks, coughing and spluttering as they tried to clear the water from their eyes.

Alex, Li and Paulo all turned to see where

the water had come from. Heather was standing there, holding a dripping bucket. She seemed to crackle with a furious energy. The freckles stood out darkly on her white face and the muscles jumped in her clenched jaw. She threw the bucket to the deck, where it rolled backwards and forwards with a metallic rumbling in the sudden silence. Heather let the silence grow until she had their full attention. When she finally spoke, her voice was tight and small, as though she was holding back a roar.

'Clean up this mess, then report to me on the aft-deck in ten minutes,' she snapped, then strode away without looking back.

About the Author

CHRIS RYAN joined the SAS in 1984 and has been involved in numerous operations with the Regiment. During the first Gulf War he was the only member of an eight-man team to escape from Iraq, three colleagues being killed and four captured. It was the longest escape and evasion in the history of the SAS. For this he was awarded the Military Medal. He wrote about his remarkable escape in *The One Who Got Away* (1995), which was also adapted for screen.

He left the SAS in 1994 and is now the author of many bestselling thrillers for adults, as well as the *Alpha Force* series for younger readers. His work in security takes him around the world and he has also appeared in a number of television series, including *Hunting Chris Ryan*, in which his escape and evasion skills were demonstrated to the max, and *Pushed to the Limit*, in which Chris put ordinary British families through a series of challenges. More recently, he appeared in *Terror Alert* on Sky TV, demonstrating his skills in a range of different scenarios.

Flash Flood is the first in a new series of adventures for younger readers.

ALPHA FORCE – THE MISSIONS
Have you read them all . . . ?

SURVIVAL The five members of Alpha Force meet for the first time when they survive a shipwreck and are marooned on a desert island.

RAT-CATCHER Alpha Force fight to catch an evil drugs baron in South America.

DESERT PURSUIT Alpha Force come face-to-face with a gang of child-slavers operating in the Sahara Desert.

HOSTAGE When they are alerted to reports of illegal dumping of toxic waste, Alpha Force fly to Canada to investigate.

RED CENTRE An Australian bushfire and a hunted terrorist test Alpha Force's skills to the limit.

HUNTED Alpha Force find themselves in a desperate battle with a ruthless band of ivory poachers in Zambia.

BLOOD MONEY While they are in southern India, Alpha Force learn of a growing trade in organ transplants from living donors and must locate a young girl before it's too late.

FAULT LINE Disaster strikes when a massive earthquake devastates a built-up area in Belize.

BLACK GOLD Alpha Force are diving in the Caribbean when an oil tanker runs aground and when an assassin strikes they need all their skills to survive.

UNTOUCHABLE Alpha Force must unearth the truth about the mysterious activity on a laird's estate in the Scottish Highlands.

THINK YOU CAN HANDLE MORE ACTION?*

Check out Chris Ryan's action adventures for adult readers

CHRIS RYAN
Blackout

THE NO.1 BESTSELLER
CHRIS RYAN
The Increment

HIS NEW BESTSELLER
CHRIS RYAN
Greed

THE TOP TEN BESTSELLER
CHRIS RYAN
The Watchman

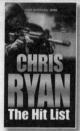

CHRIS RYAN
The Hit List

CHRIS RYAN
The Kremlin Device

ASSASSINATE THE PRIME MINISTER OR YOUR SON DIES
CHRIS RYAN
Zero Option

CHRIS RYAN
Land of Fire

CHRIS RYAN
Stand By, Stand By

CHRIS RYAN
Tenth Man Down

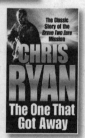

The Classic Story of the Bravo Two Zero Mission
CHRIS RYAN
The One That Got Away

*WARNING — ADULT CONTENT

AVAILABLE IN ARROW PAPERBACK

WIN A HELICOPTER LESSON!

How many of your friends can actually say they have flown a helicopter?

Now's the chance to be the envy of everyone you know by taking to the skies with aviation's coolest sport!

The hour long lesson includes a pre-flight briefing with your instructor and then a 25 minute flight where you will be able to take the controls and fly the helicopter. Wearing headphones – so you can listen to your instructor and Air Traffic Control – you will look, feel and BE the part of a real helicopter pilot! Good luck!

HOW TO ENTER:

Simply write your name, address, age, and e-mail address on a postcard and send it to:

**Marketing Department (TC),
Random House Children's Books,
61–63 Uxbridge Road, London W5 5SA.**

By 30th September 2006

To sign up for our monthly e-mail newsletter for news of brand new titles and exclusive competitions, simply write the word **NEWSLETTER** on your entry.